HANDLINER'S ISLAND

HANDLINER'S ISLAND

Arthur Mayse

Illustrated by Nola Johnston

HARBOUR PUBLISHING

Harbour Publishing Co. Ltd.
P.O. Box 219
Madeira Park, BC
Canada V0N 2H0

Canadian Cataloguing in Publication Data

Mayse, Arthur, 1912–
  Handliner's island

  ISBN 1-55017-025-2

  I. Title.
PS8576.A97H3 1990   jC813'.54   C90-091595-1
PZ7.M39Ha 1990

Jacket design by Roger Handling
Jacket illustration by Nola Johnston
Author photo by Paul Bailey / Deadeye Photography
Printed and bound in Canada by Friesen Printers

For
Win

Contents

1

Needed: A Summer Stake

Big Joe Busby shook his head. Joe was the manager of Bukwis Island cannery, and normally a pleasant, easy-going operator. But while Paddy Logan laid it out for him, Joe kept shaking his head like a metronome in a side-to-side negative.

"I'm sorry," he said to Paddy and to Paddy's Kwakiutl Indian friend, George Mayus Simon, who stood dark and brooding beside him. "Real sorry, boys. It's just that you're too young. Was I to give you jobs, I'd have the union and the labour department and Lord knows who-all on my tail."

"Not even part-time jobs?" Paddy asked. Then, earnestly, "I've just got to make some money!"

"Let's see now," said Joe. His eyes squinted. Concentrating hard, he gazed out along the cannery dock to the peacock blue and green of Bukwis Channel. "How about if you was to go clam-digging? I figure Inspector Gillies, the Fisheries chief, would give you permits."

"How much would that pay us?" Mayus put in.

Joe did some mental calculating. "Near as I can figure," he said, "If you worked hard, you might make a hundred, maybe a hundred-fifty bucks before school goes in."

"Not enough," Paddy said promptly, while his heart sank closer to his runners. "I've got to have eight hundred dollars."

Joe stared at him. "Holy old baldheaded! What's a thirteen-year-old kid need that kind of stake for?"

"It isn't me that needs it," Paddy said. "It's my grandpa. With him not being too well this last year and the interest going so high, he can't keep up with his mortgage payments. If he had eight hundred dollars, he could make do until his young steers are ready for market. If he can't raise it . . ."

His voice trailed off. Joe Busby finished for him. "He stands to lose his ranch, huh? That's rough."

Paddy nodded, not trusting his voice. Back of his eyes was a vision of the British Columbia coast stump ranch to which he came from his Washington State home each year to spend his long vacation. There was the house, old, foursquare, with weathered paint and broad verandah. The big vegetable garden out back, the hen run and outhouses, the steer-dotted pastures rolling from the edge of the evergreen woods to the rocky shoreline. The ranch meant a lot to his grandfather, and to him, too. Life wouldn't be the same if old Bruce Logan lost it all because a bank foreclosed on him.

Big Joe considered, fingers hooked in his belt, eyes narrowed against the sun-glare.

"Y'know," he said, "there's a kid, a girl about your age, does pretty well handlining for salmon. Old Ben Hutchins is her granddad. He was a rowboat fisherman from away back, he taught Lynn all the tricks of the trade."

Another thoughtful pause. "If you fellas can promote

yourselves a couple of boats and a bit of gear, you might try handlining."

Paddy shot a dubious glance at Mayus.

"This girl," Mayus asked, "this Lynn Hutchins, how much does she make?"

Joe Busby considered, lips pursed. "Well, right now, not much more'n enough to keep her and her grandpa in groceries. But if there's a real good coho salmon run, she could make the kind of money you're needing."

"Pretty much of a gamble, isn't it?" Paddy asked.

"Sure is," Joe said. "I'll be honest with you boys. There hasn't been that kind of coho run for years. Still, it's the only way you might make a quick killin' that I can come up with."

"We'll think about it," Paddy said, without much conviction.

"Sure," Joe said. "You do that." A grin quirked his lips. "Anyhow, you'll be safe from ol' Bukwis among the islands, eh, Mayus?"

Joe Busby sauntered back into the shadowy cavern of the cannery. Paddy, tall, angular and sandy-topped, and Mayus, short and sturdy, mooched off along the dock with hands shoved into jeans pockets.

Although they weren't in a mood to appreciate the fact, it was a royal day in this summer of 1946 . . . the kind that June can bring to the British Columbia coast of Canada. The weather, dour and changeable all through the North Pacific spring, had settled at last into a succession of hot blue-and-gold days. A light westerly flecked the passage between the crowding green islands with white. Puffball clouds, an armada of them, cruised along the eastern horizon above the mainland peaks; the arching dome of sky between was faintly rimmed with bronze.

Beside Mayus, in the ancient truck that the Kwakiutl

boy had persuaded his grandfather, Chief Simon, to buy, Paddy considered his situation.

The war was over. The world had turned once more to the problems of peace. And one of these cast its dark shadow over Paddy's happiness. Next year Bruce Logan's ranch might be in other hands, and no longer his to return to for a summer in Canada. Somehow he had to earn what seemed to him an earth-shaking sum.

Paddy broke out of his gloomy thoughts. He poked Mayus with an elbow.

"Listen," he asked. "Who is this Bukwis?"

Mayus gave him an abstracted answer. At the moment, Mayus was far removed in spirit from the frolicsome racoon which his Kwakiutl name, bestowed at a long-ago potlatch gathering of the bands, signified. "Huh? Bukwis? Wild man of the woods, the old people call him. This is s'posed to be his island. He's one to watch out for."

Later, lying in his bed in the upstairs room which had been his island-born father's as a boy, Paddy bludgeoned his brains for a solution other than the way-out one Joe Busby had proposed. "Go handlining," Joe had suggested, but that was so much garbage! Okay for the days before the war maybe, away back when life was simpler. Today, even gas-fueled boats were vanishing from the salmon grounds. It was all big diesel-powered trollers now, complex fishing machines like his friend Gus Sorensen's *Westerly*.

Paddy let the notion slip away. He slept like a log until the sound of his grandfather's clattering around in the kitchen roused him to yet another hot day of a summer that was moving along too quickly.

2

Paddy Makes a Decision

Paddy found his grandfather grim and short-spoken. The reason was not hard to discover. Dropped on the kitchen table was a letter from the thin sheaf of mail which Paddy had picked up at the cannery yesterday. Paddy spotted it as he turned away from the big black range with the coffee pot in his fist. The envelope carried the bank's name and logo.

He itched to know what the letter said. But a glance at Bruce Logan's face with its deep-grooved frown made him decide it would be the better part of wisdom to ignore the letter. Paddy slopped coffee into his mug, tipped a couple of fried eggs and four strips of bacon out of the vast frying pan onto his plate, and crossed to the table.

They ate with a minimum of conversation.

Once Bruce Logan said, "Taties need hilling." And again, with a rat-trap snap, "Manners, lad! Ye're not a starving wolf. I'll thank ye to eat like a Christian."

"Sorry, Grandpa," Paddy said meekly. He mopped up his plate with the last of his toast, then took himself off outside into a morning that gave promise of another hot day shaping up.

He was halfway down his first row of potato plants, shirt off and hoe busy drawing earth into heaps around each sturdy green leaf-cluster, when he heard the melancholy drone and wail of his grandfather's bagpipes from the farmhouse.

Paddy recognized the air: Bruce Logan was piping "MacRimmon's Lament."

He's playing to keep his courage up. The thought flicked coldly across his consciousness. *That letter from the bank was bad news . . .*

When he did venture to ask his grandfather at lunchtime, Bruce Logan gave a gruff answer.

"Ah," he said, "they havered to an' fro an' roundabout. Then they decided they couldna' gie me a six-month extension on my loan." He pushed his half-finished bowl of stew away. "But they've gi'en me two months at least, so the Lord be thankit!"

"Two months?" Paddy echoed the words in quick dismay. "Gee, Grandpa, that isn't long!"

Bruce Logan's mouth tightened into a humourless smile.

"Perhaps a miracle will happen," he said. "Only I dinna' take much stock in miracles."

Paddy's concern deepened. For his grandfather to lose the ranch . . . a wild kingdom that he too had learned to love . . . why, that was unthinkable! Somehow, he must find a way to come up with the money. But how? The question continued to bedevil him.

They washed their dishes in silence. Then Bruce Logan clumped up the stairs to his room for the after-lunch rest which his doctor had decreed. With a heavy heart, Paddy returned to his potato hilling.

He finished that row, but instead of starting another, stood leaning on his hoe while his thoughts moved in futile circles, like a chipmunk on a wheel.

His eyes, unseeing, gazed downslope to the cove and to the passage beyond. As he stared, a twinkle of bright silver engaged his vision. It flashed again, and yet again. Out there in the tideway, an early-run coho salmon had jumped lonely and lordly, hurling itself high out of the saltchuck. Was that fish trying to tell him something?

If some stupid girl could make a go of handlining for salmon, why couldn't he?

It was a crazy notion...a long shot...the chances heavily against him making what seemed like an appallingly large sum. But he had a rowboat, and he could scrape up a few dollars for gear, and it was the only chance...

Paddy dropped his hoe between potato rows. He set off, running, for the height-of-land that sloped down on its far side to the Indian reserve.

He was panting like a half-foundered horse when he turned into the nettle-bordered path that led to the front door of Chief Simon's weatherbeaten cedar-siding house above the reserve cove.

Mrs. Simon received him kindly, with a smile on her broad brown face.

"Come and sit," she bade Paddy. "Mayus'll be in pretty soon."

The chief sat in his half-barrel armchair alongside the stove, a slip of yellow alderwood across his knees. With a crooked knife fitted to a deerhorn handle, Chief Simon was carving a ladle. Its deeply-dished bowl was already finished. Now, one delicate shaving at a time, he was at work on the handle, where a totem in a miniature was emerging from the wood. Paddy recognized Thunderbird at the top, and under him, Beaver, distinguished by a broad, flat tail and enormous incisors.

Mrs. Simon brought Paddy a plate on which sat a plump section of golden-brown bannock, fresh from the stove and dripping with honey. Then she offered a mug of strong, heavily-sugared tea.

It was Paddy's first call of the summer on his Kwakiutl friends. After all, he had only arrived at the ranch last week. He accepted the treat gratefully, hungry again in spite of his lunchtime stew. Munching, he watched Chief Simon's big scarred hand guiding the knife.

The chief spoke out of silence, startling him.

"I'm sorry to hear about your grandpa's trouble, boy," he said in his heavy voice. "I wish there was a way we could help him."

"I'm going to do that," Paddy said. "I'm going handlining for salmon."

Having put words to the idea, he found that it took on substance and reality. The realization brought a gone feeling to the pit of his stomach. He'd said it: he was committed.

Chief Simon, hands deliberate, laid his carving on the table beside him. He considered, a chunky, weathered old man in Bannockburn tweed pants and heavy-knit Indian sweater patterned front and back with killer whales.

"Handlining, is it?" he said. "Only one person I know of goes handlining these days."

"Sure," Paddy said. "I know. Some girl."

A trace of a smile stirred Chief Simon's grey walrus moustache.

"Lynn Hutchins," he said. "Pretty smart girl, seems like."

The door banged open. In tramped Mayus, firewood piled so high in his arms that only his roach of stiff black hair showed above his load. He blundered his way to the box by the stove and dropped his wood with a crash. Then he turned grinning to Paddy.

"Okay," he said. "When do we start?"

"Start what?" Paddy demanded.

"Handlining, stupid," Mayus said. "That's what I heard you talking about through the window, wasn't it?"

Chief Simon raised a restraining hand.

"Hold up." he said. "Not so fast! You better pick your place, and make certain sure Joe Busby will buy from you before you go flyin' off. Better see to your boats, too. You need a sound boat for that game."

"Sure," Paddy said. Now that they'd made a decision, he was on fire to begin. "Only, where should we head for, Chief Simon?"

"Lemme study on that," the chief said. A frown between his deepset eyes, he considered. A hand rose to stroke absently at his grizzled moustache.

"If it was me," he said finally, "I'd hole up on Diablo Island. Used to be a handliners' camp there before the war. Diablo's on the salmon track, an' she's near enough so you can row across to the cannery with your fish."

"Sounds great," said Paddy with cheerful brashness. He swigged down his tea, crammed the last of his bannock into his mouth, and bounced to his feet. Around the bannock, he said to Mayus, "What are we waiting for? Let's get going!"

Mayus hesitated. He looked pleadingly at his grandmother, then at the chief.

Mrs. Simon smiled. She answered Mayus's unspoken question. "All right, I know you're eating your heart out to shack up on Diablo. Only you'll have to keep in touch, hear?"

The chief gazed solemnly at the boys. But the smile crinkles had deepened around his eyes.

"Yeah," he said. "I guess you better go along, Grandson. Keep this Yankee greenhorn out of trouble."

Outside, trotting down toward the reserve cove where

Mayus's slim black dugout canoe lay drawn up on the beach, Paddy felt considerably lighter in his spirits. It helped too—helped a lot—that Mayus was going to partner up with him for the adventure. Maybe it was a screwy idea. Maybe, in fact more than likely, they'd fall on their noses. But at least it was something they could get going on, and that was infinitely better than sitting on his hands and worrying.

Mayus's voice brought him back to the realities.

"We got a heck of a lot to do," Mayus said. "Those boats are goin' to need plenty work."

For the rest of that day, they toiled over Mayus's canoe, a graceful fifteen-footer shaped and hollowed from a single cedar log. A split had opened in the bottom of the fragile craft; they cut a patch from the side of a five-gallon fuel can with tinsnips borrowed from Bruce Logan's toolshed, found a trove of copper boat nails, and gave the split section a protective sheathing both inside and out. Then they heated tar over a beach fire and, daubing it on smoking hot, sealed their patches.

Lastly, they laid on a coat of black paint to match the outside of the hull, and found a smidgen of green in an ancient can for the interior.

"Now we'll start on your boat," Mayus said as he rubbed his hands briskly on his jeans.

But Paddy declined. "I've had it," he said. "My tongue's hanging out. We'll get after my boat tomorrow."

Still scrubbing, Mayus scowled at his friend.

"Listen," he said, "those coho salmon could be showing up off Diablo any day now. An' we need to be there when they put in!"

3

The Black Seiner

For much of the next day, they laboured over Paddy's ancient flat-bottomed skiff with melted tar and oakum frayed from tags of old rope. Paddy applied the last lick of tar to a seam. Sweating in the keen July sunlight, bare shoulders already brown under their shreds of peeling skin from his first sunburn, he rocked back on his heels.

"The *Spotted Dog*," he said, surveying his work with a critical eye. "That's what I'll call her."

"Well," Mayus said, jamming his swab back into the tar can, "We're not finished yet. Now we ought to plim her."

"Plim her?" Paddy asked. "What's that?"

"Sink her in the chuck," Mayus told him. "Load her with rocks to hold her under, an' let her soak for two-three days. That way she'll be certain not to leak."

They skidded the skiff down to the shallows. There they tipped it on its side, letting it fill with water, and were piling in rocks to hold it on the bottom when Mayus swivelled his head around.

"Oh boy!" It was a sharp exclamation of dismay. "Look out there."

Paddy looked. A chunky, ugly vessel lay off the north point that guarded the creek mouth. It was dingy black in colour. On a drum mounted in its waist was a mass of green netting speckled with the white of plastic floats.

Mayus studied the black fishboat, face set in a scowl that tugged his mouth corners down.

"What's the trouble?" Paddy asked him.

"They're the trouble," Mayus said. He jerked his chin at the two men who lounged against the boat's deck-house, looking shoreward. "You know who those fellas are?"

Paddy shook his head. One of the pair on the black boat, he could make out, was tall and heavy-shouldered, with flaming red hair. The other, older man was bald as an egg except for a tuft by each ear that gave him the look of a horned owl.

"That big guy," Mayus said, "he's Red Dunc Sloan. The other's his sidekick, Arnie Peters." Mayus heaved up a rock and dropped it into the swamped skiff, splashing them both. "Those two," he said, "are the meanest creek robbers in these parts."

"Creek robbers?"

"Yeah. They wait till a drove of salmon is packed into a creek mouth waiting for rain so they can go up-river to spawn. Then they move in with a short net like the one they have on that seine-drum and make a hurry-up set. One good score an' they've cleaned out a whole year's run of salmon."

"What happens if they're caught?" Paddy asked, eyes squinted the better to make out the faces of the men on the black seiner.

"*If* they're caught," said Mayus, "Fisheries grabs their nets an' socks 'em with a fine. Prob'ly takes their boat

away, too. Ol' Inspector Gillies is real tough with people that break the law."

"Well, I can't see them doing much harm here," Paddy observed. "There's no salmon in the creek."

"Not yet," Mayus said grimly. He climbed to his feet; his scowl darkened. "Only any day now a run of early humpbacks will hit the creek. That's what those no-goods are up to. Keepin' an eye out for that humpy run." He added in vindictive tones, "Would I ever like to see Inspector Gillies light on their tails!"

Paddy deposited a final stone in the skiff's bows. Trailing the painter hooked to a ring in the skiff's nose, he crunched back up the beach. "What's to stop us turning them in?" he asked Mayus.

Mayus gaped at him in horror.

"We can't do that!" he said sharply. "Nobody ever turns anyone in to the Fisheries guys. That'd be finking."

"All right, all right," Paddy said. "Only I think if they're poachers somebody ought to blow the whistle on them."

The two men in the black seiner were launching their net-skiff. It slid into the water. Red Dunc dropped to the bottomboards and settled himself on a thwart. He lifted oar looms into rowlocks and unhurriedly stroked his way into the creek mouth.

"We better get out of here," Mayus muttered.

"Why?"

"Red Dunc's a tough operator," Mayus said. "Just as well if he don't know we've spotted him.

Still Paddy lingered. He had cooked up a considerable dislike for the big redheaded poacher and his bald partner.

"Come on!" Mayus tugged urgently at his arm. "Jeez, ain't you got any sense?"

He tugged Paddy into the brush screen. Red Dunc had

eased off his rowing and was staring intently in the boys' direction.

Walking fast, Mayus headed along the trail that led to his home reserve.

Paddy tagged after him. His hackles were still up; he resented the impudence of fish thieves putting into his home cove, his particular creek mouth.

"I still think we should do something about this," he said.

"I'll tell you what to do," Mayus said over his shoulder. "Forget you ever saw 'em!"

But Paddy had no intention of forgetting. Maybe it went against the upcoast code to tip off the Fisheries officers when creek robbers were on the prowl. But it occurred to Paddy that there might be other ways to put a crimp in their operation.

Once on the reserve's single beach-fronting road, Mayus strode purposefully toward Chief Simon's rattletrap truck which he piloted to and fro between home and cannery without benefit of license.

"Where now?" Paddy asked.

"Cannery store," Mayus said. It was plain that he was still upset over the near-confrontation at the cove. "If we're goin' handlining, we'll need gear, won't we?" As an afterthought, swinging into the cab truck, he added, "I hope you've got some money."

They blew a tire on the way to the store. By the time they'd changed it for a spare in not much better condition, the afternoon was well along.

In the store, they found sharp-nosed, sharp-tongued Mrs. Busby weighing rice out of a sack for a customer.

This was a girl, short and sturdy, with a close-cropped helmet of cedarwood-coloured hair. Her jeans were patched and faded, her arms and face tanned to a biscuit brown. Green eyes gave Paddy and Mayus a cool appraisal as they stepped up to the counter.

"Hi, Lynn," Mayus greeted her.

The girl—she looked to be about Paddy's age—nodded. She said to Mayus, ignoring Paddy, "I hear you plan to go handlining." Her tone was as cool as her gaze.

"How'd you know that?" Paddy challenged her. At the moment, he wasn't over-partial to redheads.

"Joe Busby told me," the girl said. Then, dropping her words deliberately, "I wouldn't, if I were you."

"Why not?" Paddy demanded.

The girl let herself become aware of his existence. Her green eyes studied him. She had, he noticed, a faint peppering of freckles across her nose. She said in the same deliberate way, "Because you'd drown yourselves or go broke. Or both."

Lynn turned her back on them. She lifted her brown paper sack of purchases from the counter, said, "Thanks, Mrs. Busby," and started for the door.

"Say hello to your grandpa for me," Mrs. Busby called after her. "And tell him to stop by sometime."

That dictum delivered, Mrs. Busby hitched her short, square self around to front Paddy and Mayus.

"All right, you two," she said briskly. "What's it going to be?"

They bought a hank of sturdy white seine twine to be cut into handlines, and a bag of the brown dye which Mayus called "kutch" to stain it. Then a coil of thin, springy piano wire was needed to make leaders that would run between lines and lures to serve as camouflage.

Swivels, snap connectors and sinkers in weights to a couple of pounds joined their plunder on the counter. Last came a selection of spoons . . . shiny silver and brass-finished lures, slim and streamlined, in sizes from three to six inches long. Each spoon was armed with a needle-pointed Pacific salmon hook of blued steel.

"We better have some spare hooks," Mayus told Paddy, "an' we'll need gaffs."

They added gaff-hooks to be lashed to wooden handles and used for swinging their catches on board.

"There!" Paddy announced with a good deal of satisfaction. "I guess that's the works."

He tugged out his pocketbook. Most of his newspaper route money had gone for new skis last winter and for a racing bike this spring. He was two dollars short of the thirty-five needed to cover their bill.

"We'll carry it on the books," Mrs. Busby told them. She added briskly, "There'll be interest, of course."

Mayus was dredging in his jeans. Grinning, he fetched out a crumpled five-dollar bill, which he laid with Paddy's contribution on the counter.

"Birthday present from my grandpa," he explained, "so we start with the books clear."

They carried their gear out to the dock. At a float that lay chained close in to the dock pilings, Lynn Hutchins was stepping into a slim green double-ended rowboat. She settled herself on the middle thwart, reached for the oars, then looked up at Paddy and Mayus, her dark face unsmiling.

"Got your commercial fishing licences yet?" she called up to them. "Or did you forget about that?"

I'm not going to fight with her, Paddy told himself. *No point.*

He said to Lynn, "Thanks for reminding us. We'll look after that right now."

"Well, good luck," Lynn said. She did smile then, a brief and humourless quirking of her mouth. "You may need it."

With an oar, she pushed her boat away from the float. Then, stroking easily, she headed into the channel.

Mayus, frowning, stared after her. "Prickly as a sea-urchin," he said. "Now what'd she mean by that?"

"Don't know," Paddy said. He settled the sack of gear under his arm. "But we'd better go see about those licences."

They found Inspector Gillies up to his ears in paperwork, below decks in the trim grey Fisheries cruiser that lay snugged to her lines alongside the cannery float string.

"You picked a bad day, boys," warned the crewman who nodded them down the companion. "The Old Man's just lost a court case at Powell River. Loggers draglining through a creek spawning bed...thought he'd nailed 'em for sure!"

The crewman left them outside the cabin door.

Paddy tapped. A crisp voice called, "Come in."

Inspector Gillies was lean, trim and precise, with a weathered hatchet face and hard pale blue eyes. He heard Paddy out, then shook his head.

"Sorry. You're wasting your time. Nobody goes handlining any more."

"Lynn Hutchins does," Mayus said.

"We make an exception in her case," the inspector said crisply. "She knows the ropes, learned them from her grandfather."

"We'd still like to try it," Paddy said. He added a belated, "Sir."

Inspector Gillies leaned back in his chair, brown hands on his desk.

"I'm sorry," he said with a dismaying air of finality. "I can't oblige you. This is no water for a couple of green young boys to be fooling about on. Try again when you're a couple of years older. Meanwhile, I'd suggest you lads look for some easier and safer way to make a dollar."

Paddy, heart somewhere down around his knees, mounted the companion and stepped out to the float.

"Okay," Mayus said glumly. "I guess that's that." Then, as Paddy strode off along the dock, "Hey . . . where you goin'?"

Paddy didn't answer. He was bitterly disappointed. In spite of his reservations about the practicality of handlining, it had offered at least a chance to make the summer stake he so badly needed. Now that prospect was blasted. They were left with a mess of fishing gear that he could only hope the store would take back, and with egg all over their faces. Even so, there was a thing which he felt, as a matter of duty, needed doing.

He tossed Mayus a delayed answer to his question as his friend trotted up level with him.

"I'm going to tell Gus Sorensen about those creek robbers."

They found Gus squatting cross-legged on his troller's after-hatch cover with a coil of rope draped over his knees and a splicing fid in his fist.

"Hello, kid," he greeted Paddy. It was Gus who had given Paddy a hitch north from Powell River when he came up to start his summer vacation. In the course of the run, they'd become friends. "Haven't seen you for a coon's age . . . How goes it?"

Gus looked up with his easy smile, a grin that faded as he studied Paddy's face. He answered his own question. "Not so good, huh?"

"That old Inspector Gillies," Paddy grumbled. "He won't give us commercial licenses so we can go handlining. Says we're too young.

He stepped down into Gus Sorensen's *Westerly*, liking the feel of the tall-poled troller under his feet. Funny— even to be in a boat raised his spirits a little.

"That's the God's truth," Gus said, poking his sharp-pointed fid under a rope strand of the long-splice he was building.

"Anyway," Paddy said, "that's how it is." He made a change of subject. "Hey, Gus, something came up we thought you should know about. There's creek robbers hanging around the mouth of Cormorant Creek."

Gus's blonde head lifted from his work. He gave Paddy a sharp scrutiny.

"You sure of that?"

"Yeah," Mayus put in. "It's Arnie Peters and Red Dunc Sloan."

Gus whistled softly. "Them two, eh?" He tumbled the rope off his knees and uncoiled his long frame. For a moment he loomed in his familiar, spraddle-legged slouch, thumbs in his belt. A frown tugged his sandy eyebrows together.

"Crick busters from awayback," Gus growled. "I don't know how many runs they've killed stone cold dead. Us trollermen don't owe them thieves anything except..."

Gus let what he was about to say trail off into nothing. Then, with an air of decision, he spoke again.

"Tell you what, boys. S'pose you keep an eye on the crick-mouth. 'Specially around evening when tide's in an' dark's just starting to haul down. If Arnie an' Red Dunc move in, you light out for the cannery. Shoot me the word real fast, understand?"

Paddy said, "Will do, Gus." Mayus nodded an affirmative. They left Gus to his splicing and rattled out along the island road in Mayus's pickup.

They didn't talk. Disappointment over the inspector's turndown still weighed heavily upon them.

At supper, a meal which Paddy normally tackled with wolfish appetite, he merely picked at his plate of ground meat and home-canned peas served with potatoes from his grandfather's root cellar.

Bruce Logan gave his grandson a searching survey. The old man's eyes, very blue and clear, were still startlingly youthful. But the rest of him—and this Paddy admitted with an inward pang—was showing his seventy-six years. Too old to be pestered with such worries as mortgage payments he couldn't meet.

"Now what's amiss?" Bruce Logan demanded. "Dinna' tell me ye've had anither falling-out wi' yer friend off the resairve."

"Nothing like that, Grandpa," Paddy assured him. He transferred a forkful of meat to his mouth: it was tender, and he had to admit, very tasty. "What's this we're eating tonight? Veal?"

"Young cat," his grandfather said.

"*Cat?*" Paddy checked his fork midway to his mouth.

"Cougar, boy, cougar," Bruce Logan said. His face, severely lined under its crest of white hair, creased in a smile.

"Aye," he said, "yon saucy beast came strollin' doon the auld logging road one evening wi' his hands in his pockets, ye might say. Ready to jump one o' my calves, did the chance offer. I was out after grouse, but it chanced I had a buckshot load handy'by. I kept the best of him for my freezer. Made a nice wee sum sellin' the hairt an' whiskers to the Chinese at the cannery. They claim there's virtue in those, the puir misguided heathen!"

But Bruce Logan was not to be put off the track. He returned to his earlier question. "I asked what ails ye, laddy?"

Paddy told him. He had not expected the old man to sympathize, but he had failed to reckon with clan loyalty. Bruce Logan bristled on his behalf, taking the inspector's refusal of a fishing license only less hard than he.

"Outrageous!" he snapped. "I'll be havin' a word wi' Angus Gillies. Ye may be sure I'll gie him a piece o' my mind!"

4

The Creek Robbers

There matters rested. The long, hot days followed on each other's heels. June was slipping all too fast toward July. Paddy kept himself busy. He was filling a bucket with green peas in the big, deer-fenced vegetable garden one evening when Mayus came tearing lickety-split from the direction of the rock point that lay between Bruce Logan's farm and the reserve.

Mayus sent his voice ahead of him.

"They're here!" he called. "They've put in!"

"Who?" Arnie Peters and Red Dunc Sloan had been far from his thoughts.

"The creek robbers." Mayus hauled up, panting. "Come on. I left the truck up on the road. They're right in the creek mouth, putting a skiff over."

Paddy left his bucket of peas sitting between rows. He raced after Mayus out to the dirt road where the pickup waited with engine wheezing.

"Didn't want to turn her off," Mayus explained as they scrambled into the cab. "She mightn't have started again."

Even though Mayus drove with accelerator jammed to the floorboards, the slow old truck seemed to take forever to cover the four miles to Bukwis Island cannery.

Mayus sent the pickup bucking and jolting over the dock planking, to slam to a halt opposite the float string. Gus was in port: his *Westerly* lay to her lines alongside the middle float. Paddy and Mayus boiled out and down to the troller at a run.

They found Gus in his tiny galley, a halibut hash sizzling in his big black iron frying pan.

Regretfully, Gus shoved the pan to the back of his stove. He monkeyed up the companion and hailed *Ocean Breeze*, a stately offshore troller tied next in line.

"Hey! Ollie! We got a bone to pick."

Olav Larson, a blocky Swede, poked his head from his wheelhouse.

"Them crick robbers, yah?" he acknowledged in his chesty bellow.

Paddy heard *Ocean Breeze*'s heavy-duty diesel rumble into life at the thrust of Ollie's thumb on the starter.

Ollie hollered over the throaty engine-song to the smaller troller tied abreast.

"Yo! *Wonder Girl*! Rouse up, Toivo. . . creek robbers!"

Already, Gus was freeing Westerly's lines.

"Can we come with you?" Paddy put the question eagerly to Gus.

"Not a chance." Gus flashed him a grin. "Party's likely to turn rough. You kids keep right outa the way, see?"

From the dock, regretfully, Paddy and Mayus watched the three trollers, tall main-poles triced up beside their stubby masts, line out through the cannery cove mouth. They dwindled swiftly out of sight around the first rocky headland.

Paddy sighed. "Just our luck," he muttered. "We're missing all the fun."

"Fun?" Mayus fell into step beside him. They started back to the truck. "You call that fun? Listen, those fellas play real tough."

On the trip back to the reserve, the truck blew another tire. The spare was still waiting in Chief Simon's woodshed to be patched. They limped on toward home with rope wound around the rim: their progress was excruciatingly slow. When they did pull to a steaming halt outside the chief's house, black dark had fallen.

"Come on," Paddy said. "Let's go over to Cormorant Cove for a look-see."

Cautiously, they felt their way down the creekside trail. Where the woods thinned ahead, Mayus flung out a restraining hand to check Paddy, who blundered at his heels.

Through a thinning screen of brush, they could see the ruddy glow of a fire on the cove beach.

They ventured on a step at a time until the woods released them.

Dim in the starlit cove, the three trollers rode at anchor above their own shadowy reflections. Of the black drum-seiner, there was no sign.

Dark against the glow of the flame, a tall figure heaved more driftwood on the fire. Sparks rose in a shower. By their light, Paddy could see that the man was Gus.

He and Mayus crunched along the clamshell beach and into the firelit circle.

Gus hailed them cheerfully.

"Couldn't stay away, huh? Well, you missed the party."

Only then did Paddy observe that the fire owed no small part of its glow to the pile of treated netting that burned busily with random spurts of flame.

Paddy also saw that Gus's left cheekbone was raw-red as if abraded by some hard object, and that the knuckles on both of big Ollie's ham-like fists were skinned.

But it would not be politic, Paddy decided, to ask any questions.

Nevertheless, Gus tossed him an oblique answer.

"Those hoosiers won't raid any more cricks for a spell," he said.

Toivo Eliasen, lean skipper of the *Wonder Girl*, nodded. His smile was wolfish.

"You can count on that, you bet!" Toivo said. "Them *perikeltes* won't bother anyone for a while."

"What's 'per...perikelte', Toivo?" Paddy asked, challenged as always by a strange new word.

Toivo smiled at him, his hard cheekbones standing out like knobs in the fireglow. "In Finland," he said, "where I come from, we have three devils, each one meaner than the last. Perikelte, that's the meanest of them all."

The klatch around the fire expanded into an impromptu party. Gus rowed out to *Westerly* for his monstrous halibut hash, which he brought ashore to reheat in the embers of their fire.

Ollie supplied coffee, fiercely strong, and Toivo raided his ship's lockers for a couple of over-age bakery pies and a bottle of brown Demarara rum.

"None for you kids," Gus said severely as he laced his, Ollie's and Toivo's mugs of coffee. "You got to grow up first."

"Even then," said Ollie virtuously, "better if you let the stuff alone."

"By rights," Gus said, "you shouldn't even be drinkin' this." He gestured to the steaming enamelware coffee pot. "It's gonna stunt your growth."

For once, though, Paddy didn't mind not being grown up. Mug in fist, munching flinty pie-crust, he felt right and good for the first time since the inspector had so summarily rejected their bid for fishing licenses. Strong in him was the feeling that he was among friends.

Only when the fire was low, and when Ollie and Toivo

were launching their dinghies in the star-mirroring cove, Gus dropped a warning.

"I doubt anything'll come of this," he said, his tone casual, "but I got a hunch Red Dunc an' Arnie know you boys turned 'em in. Red Dunc said something to Arnie when we was...uh...seeing them off, about a couple of punks hangin' around spying on them." Gus splashed into the cove. His white dinghy rolled as he hoisted himself inboard and reached for his oars. "Just in case," he said, "you fellas better stay catty, eh?"

A couple of mornings later, Paddy looked down-slope through a tracery of scarlet-flowered bean vines to see a trim dove-grey launch glide around the rock point and into Cormorant Cove.

The launch ran off its way. A crewman hustled to the foredeck and lowered the anchor. The cruiser, government in every inch of its forty feet, swung to its hook with the red ensign of Canada drooping from its jackstaff in the windless heat.

Paddy, with a quickening of interest, recognized the vessel as the fisheries launch. The lean, erect man standing by while one of his crew slid a dinghy overside was Inspector Gillies.

Inspector and crewman dropped into the dinghy. With the fisheries hand at the oars and the inspector straight-backed in the stern sheets, the dinghy plodded toward the beach.

Paddy wanted to be down there. His bump of curiosity prickled; he yearned to know what had fetched the inspector here. But something mulish in his makeup kept him from downing tools and heading for the cove. He returned to his morning chore of hoeing weeds out from among the scarlet runner beans that twined up their tall stakes.

Presently he heard the garden gate creak on its hinges. Inspector Gillies and his grandfather advanced upon him.

Paddy grounded his hoe and waited, his puzzlement increasing by the second. It had to be something he'd done . . . but his conscience issued no warning jabs.

Bruce Logan cleared his throat. He spoke ceremoniously.

"Inspector Gillies here would be havin' a word wi' you."

The inspector gave Paddy a wintry hint of a smile. He said in his crisp, clipped tones, "I'll ask no questions. But I understand from information received that my department can thank you and your friend for some valuable help." He reflected a moment, looking over Paddy's head to the blue saltwater. "We haven't any salmon to waste. Certainly not spawning fish to be plundered by creek-robbers."

Paddy gulped. He brought out a non-committal, "Yessir."

"The sum of it is," the inspector said, "that I've decided to stretch a point." He drew an official-looking brown envelope from his inside jacket pocket, and handed it to Paddy.

"Here you are," he said, and the smile for a moment was remarkably human. "Don't forget to fill them in and sign them."

The inspector, with an abrupt nod, turned on his heel and started out of the garden, Bruce Logan beside him.

With fingers that trembled in spite of him, Paddy opened the envelope. It contained two rectangular forms, with the Canadian crest at the top of each. His own name leaped at him from one, Mayus's from the other.

His eyes flicked over the details: master's name, tonnage of vessel, length, beam, draft, means of propulsion . . .

What he held was a pair of commercial fishing licenses: precious documents that permitted him and Mayus to catch and sell salmon.

Paddy loosed a war-whoop that halted the inspector and Bruce Logan in their tracks. Then, clutching the licenses, he galloped out of the garden and off toward the reserve trail to share the good news with Mayus.

Bruce Logan and Inspector Gillies exchanged smiles.

"He'll do," said the inspector, and Bruce Logan nodded his head in agreement. He said, "Aye. That he will."

Then, as if he had betrayed himself by an undue display of softness, the inspector quenched his smile.

"But the law is the law," he said sternly, "and I trust your grandson will remember that. If he breaks regulations...if he gets out of line...I'll be right down his throat."

"Fair enough," said Bruce Logan equably. "Now, since yer no longer on duty, will ye be coming up tae the house to take a dram wi' me?"

5

Diablo Island

Chief Simon and his wife, Ursula, came down to the reserve beach to see Paddy and Mayus launch out. Bruce Logan was there too: he had given each boy a pair of light, beautifully-finished spoonblade oars, fashioned from straight-grained spruce in his ranch workshed.

He brushed their thanks aside. "Ye'll grow sick o' the sight of them, I make no doubt," he said dryly. "Now, be off wi' ye."

The chief wore his button-patterned dance cape of red and blue stroud. A band of twisted, red-dyed cedar bark circled his hair.

Solemnly, the chief pressed similar bark bands over Mayus's hair, then Paddy's.

"For luck," he said, "and to remind you that you belong to our family."

Ursula Simon began to chant in minor key. It was a measured refrain with sadness in it. Paddy caught the word, "Halakasla" many times repeated.

"What's that mean? 'Halakasla'?" he asked Mayus as

they rowed boat-by-boat with easy dips of their oars toward the cove entrance.

"Kind of hard to put into white man's talk," Mayus told him. He pondered for a moment, resting on his oars. "Guess it means 'Goodbye until we meet again.' Something like that."

Embarrassed, he changed the subject. "You sure we got everything?"

Paddy grinned. His skiff was deep-laden. Mayus's slim black canoe was carrying a load so heavy that its freeboard was drastically reduced.

"We sure have!" Paddy called back as the first openwater ripples of the channel set up their slap-slap under his skiff's nose.

"You remember your gun?" Mayus demanded.

But Paddy hadn't. He'd completely overlooked the little .22 singleshot rifle that had once been his father's. It still leaned in a corner of his clothes closet at the ranch with the boxes of ammunition bought for the venture stacked on the shelf above it.

"Oh well," Mayus said. "What do we need a gun for, anyhow?"

He grinned, and Paddy grinned back, glad they were under way at last.

"That's right," Paddy said. "We're going to catch salmon, not shoot 'em."

From his living-room windows, Bruce Logan watched the boats, now no more than black specks against the blue of the strait. He was going to miss Paddy, his cheerful racketing around, his enthusiasm, even his not-infrequent foolishness. It had been deeply good to have him, and to a lone and ageing man, wonderfully reassuring that his American grandson should come north to spend time with him. And now he was off on a new adventure, lighthearted and with no thought for the difficulties and even dangers involved.

. . . The dangers. Frowning, Bruce Logan continued to gaze toward the blue sea below, even though the boats had vanished from his sight.

It was an enormous, lone sea. It could be wild. Fair weather could change to foul most treacherously and with scant warning. They'd be two untried lads going up against great waters in small boats.

. . . As he had done in his own wild and hardy youth, Bruce Logan reminded himself. Time had come full circle. It was rowboat fishing that had provided the wherewithal to dig in as a rancher on Bukwis Island when he came out to Canada from Scotland, a piper discharged from a Highland regiment after the South African war. Still, that was long ago, and time changes conditions.

As he so often did when troubled, Bruce Logan turned to his pipes. He lifted the kist o' whistles from the scuffed leather armchair where he had laid them, puffed up the bag with a mental notation that it could use a good treacling, and set his fingers to the chanter.

The music welled up in him unbidden. He began to pace. . . four steps across the uncarpeted floor in front of the windows, military turn, and swagger back. . .

Perhaps he should have thrown his authority and mature judgement against the handlining venture. After all, the tricky channels of the Diablo Island group had come close as may be to drowning him. But no: he could never have stood in Paddy's way. He'd run his own risks when young, taken his chances, and his stiff sense of rectitude had kept him from interfering.

Paddy, though young enough in all conscience, had a right to meet life head-on.

Bruce Logan, only half-aware of his choice, let the

pipes lilt their way into an old boat-song of the Highlands. Words paced the music: "Carry the lad that's born tae be king, ow'er the sea to Skye."

In an hour of boat-pulling, first with the tide to help, then against its brisk flow, Diablo Island had come no closer. It lay powder-blue on the horizon, its outline blurred by heat-haze, its shape that of an air-foil with blunt leading edge butting into the path of the southeast gales.

The blisters on Paddy's palms had broken to leave raw spots that smarted with each pull on the oars. His skiff and Mayus's black canoe rode a few feet apart, dipping and lifting to the rocking-chair motion of a glassy swell.

Bukwis Island—the home-island they had left behind— was now only a dark mass to the westward, which changed shape as Paddy studied it. One minute, its rock walls were heavens high, the next, they had contracted to a narrow band against the blue. Over there on the way they had come, a mirage was working its legerdemain.

Mayus nodded toward Diablo. "You know what its Kwakwala name means?"

"Nope." Paddy answered absently, his mind occupied with long thoughts.

"Means 'Island that don't come any closer'", Mayus said. He sighed and dipped his oars. "Come on. Dig in."

It came to Paddy as they inchwormed their way on across the channel that they just might have bitten off more than they could chew. They had committed themselves to a man's undertaking. . .and they weren't men, not yet.

He realized acutely, now, that life on shore hadn't prepared him for this different and daunting world of sea and sky and distant islands into which he found himself projected. Suppose they couldn't hack it? What if they had to admit themselves licked, head back to Bukwis with their summer mostly gone and that essential eight hundred dollars still to find?

Then he remembered Lynn Hutchins, and the thought of that cool, unfriendly redhead stiffened his spine. If she could make a go of handlining, so could they. In fact, they'd probably do a lot better!

By slow and painful degrees, Diablo Island loomed larger out of the sea. Presently the boys found themsel-

ves battling a strong run of tide...a belt of turbulence that made their progress excruciatingly slow. And when the tiderip booted them into easier water, they found that their troubles were by no means over.

A little wind roved down from the northwest. At first it raised random catspaws on the humps of the rounded and evenly-spaced swells. Then a crest licked up and slopped over, showering Paddy's back with spray.

"Come on!" Mayus shouted, urgency in his tone. "Hit a lick! She's fixin' to blow."

Paddy gritted his teeth and laid into his oars. The haze had vanished. Diablo Island was now very much closer.

He judged its ramparts to be no further than a quarter-mile away. But the sea was turning uglier by the second.

The easy swell had sharpened into a succession of crested whitecaps. Paddy half-turned on the thwart to adjust the tarpaulin over his forward load so that it would be protected from flying spray. Instantly, a crester smacked hard against the skiff's right quarter, throwing her off course.

Mayus's warning yell wasn't needed. Paddy dug his oars desperately, trying to wrestle the overloaded skiff back into the teeth of the wind. One plunging oar-blade tugged against air; Paddy tumbled backward off the thwart while the skiff broached-to in the trough between steep seas.

Another violent roll. Then Paddy was in the water, fighting desperately to keep his head clear of the pyramidal seas that spired around him.

A voice penetrated his water-filled ears. "Catch hold!"

Paddy threshed with an arm, blindly grabbing. His fingers skidded off an oar-blade. Next try, he had it. His bleared eyes picked up an impression of a green rowboat beside him . . . a slim green boat with a girl at the oars.

Her voice cut at him. "All right. Hang on to the stern."

Hands locked on the green boat's pointed stern, Paddy saw Mayus juggling his canoe alongside the half-swamped skiff. Then Mayus had the painter, and with the skiff in tow, was rowing toward what seemed to be a solid wall of dark rock.

Lynn Hutchins followed, canoe and rowboat broncoing along as if the next following sea would cause them to pitch-pole end for end.

Paddy freed a hand to dash spray from his eyes. The grey rock bluffs that had seemed an unbroken wall from farther out parted to reveal a narrow gut through which

the cresters surged. Mayus put his canoe into the entrance like a horse at a gate. The canoe went surfing in
on the back of a wicked sea.

"Hang on!" Lynn's voice reached Paddy in a yelp like
a seagull's cry.

Then the rowboat climbed a surge and held there in
perilous balance. For a confused moment, the boat bob-
sledded with nose high in a rush of broken, tumbling
water. Then they were through the gut, and in a transi-
tion almost magical, floated on a saltwater lagoon which
the wind scarcely ruffled.

Paddy let his legs sag. His feet touched bottom. He
stood chest-deep on sand.

"Hey, Lynn." It came out a croak. "Thanks!"

But the green double-ender was already receding along
the lagoon, and Lynn, rowing longshore style with face
to the bows, did not bother to look back.

Feeling miserable and badly diminished, Paddy waded
toward the lagoon beach. Close by, a loon with sleek head
and speckled breast floated like a miniature battleship. A
pair of black scoters cut wakes across quiet water as they
chased each other in play. Other seafowl — gulls and
harlequin ducks, mergansers, goldeneyes and buffle-
heads — floated placidly a few feet out from a dazzling
white beach of crushed clamshell.

They had arrived at Diablo Island. But as Paddy noted
with a distinct shock, their welcome could have been
warmer.

On a point of beach that poked into the lagoon, a large
sign crudely carpentered from driftwood planks con-
fronted them from a staggering post. Crudely daubed on
the sign in red paint was a message. It warned:

KEEP OFF! TRESPASSERS WILL BE SHOT!

Mayus had grounded his canoe on the beach below the sign. The skiff lay half on its side, water draining out of it.

Paddy splashed ashore to stand by Mayus.

"Whoever put that up," Paddy said with a bravado he didn't altogether feel, "sure doesn't like people."

But Mayus didn't reply. He was staring past the sign, up the slope of golden-brown grass to where the darker line of evergreen woods began.

Silhouetted there, startling and huge, an eagle-shaped bird poised with an enormous killer whale gripped in its claws. The figure was supported on poles. It had been fashioned from cedar planks and painted in primary colours of black, red and white.

"What's that thing?" Paddy asked Mayus.

"Ah, it's just some oldtime In'yan business," Mayus answered. He continued to stare at the thunderbird and killer whale.

Paddy turned to his skiff. His oars were still there, secure in their tied-down rowlocks, but his cargo was a sorry mess. The tarp had come unshipped from the sea's clobbering. A gruel of oatmeal and saltwater swashed inches-deep in the skiff's bottom. From this turgid pool humped the big picnic ham, a product of Bruce Logan's smokehouse, that the old man had given them. Loaves of bread made other soggy islands, and a can of broached eggs added a yolk-yellow tinge to the puddle.

"Well," Paddy said, "we'd better get our stuff on shore." Even while he spoke, he noted with dismay that his tin of matches had also popped its lid and scattered its contents to float ruined in the gruel.

"I been thinking," Mayus said. "Maybe it ain't so good a notion to shack up here." He nodded at the "Keep off!" sign. "Someone could make trouble. Anyhow, if we was to camp over on Little Diablo we'd be nearer to the salmon grounds."

Paddy looked hard at his friend, startled by this sudden change of heart. Mayus's face was set in a scowl. He seemed anxious and unhappy.

"Aw, come on," Paddy said lightly. "That sign doesn't mean a thing." Then, disregarding the evidence of fresh paint, "It's prob'ly been there for years. Some joker put it up in olden days."

Paddy began to lift soaked boxes, packages and sacks out of his skiff. "Come on," he repeated. "I've got a drying-out job to do."

Mayus, his movements slow and reluctant, turned to his canoe. He too began to pile plunder on the beach.

While they worked, spreading gear and blankets to dry, and hauling the emptied boats above high tideline, they took stock of their surroundings. Scattered haphazardly along the foreshore above the crescent lagoon beach stood, or rather leaned, a straggle of tiny shacks knocked together from driftwood.

Most of them were tottering ruins, their walls open to the sky. It was obvious they hadn't been lived in for a long time.

The beach curved off in either direction to end in rugged points of reddish-coloured rock that could be volcanic in origin. Back of the shacks, across tawny downland broken by rock outcroppings, Thunderbird and Killer Whale stood guard at the edge of the woods.

Paddy turned to gaze seaward. Out there beyond the lagoon entrance, the strait was now a white lather.

I could have drowned out there...

The realization chilled him for a moment. Again, and keenly, he realized how very little he knew about the sea and its ways. But he put the thought from him. If they were going to be rowboat fishermen, hardboiled commercials out to make their stake, they couldn't afford to let a snootful of weather get them down.

"Okay," he said with exaggerated cheerfulness to Mayus, "what are we waiting for? Let's fly at it!"

Their canned goods had come through undamaged, although with most of the labels soaked off. Opening those tins was going to present an interesting form of food roulette. As for their vast ham, even though it gleamed with drying salt, it seemed impervious to damage.

Mayus hauled out his belt-knife. "I'm hungry enough to eat a shoe," he announced. He hacked off a mighty slice of ham for Paddy and another for himself. Paddy broke open a roll of only slightly damp pilot bread.

Munching, they plodded over the belt of broken clamshell toward the wild-grass flat that fronted the shacks. The silence was absolute. No creature stirred, no bird sounded off. There was only the dance-and-shimmer of heat-devils along the driftlog-strewn beach.

It occurred to Paddy, halted outside the sagging door of the shanty at the south end of the row, that he had never in all his life encountered such desolation. The island lay rocky and sun-dried, flung down in the sea . . . a strange, wild, long-forgotten place.

. . . But not altogether forgotten. Paddy corrected himself. There were Thunderbird and Killer Whale lording it at the top of the slope, and there was that hostile sign.

Paddy knew that Mayus, following close behind him, was taut as a stretched wire. There was something about this island that got under the skin: a brooding quality, a sense of waiting.

Paddy threw off the mood. He swallowed the last of his ham and turned back to the shanty.

It was ancient, and from the outside it looked to be dauntingly tumbledown. Paddy heaved at the door, which squealed open on its one protesting hinge.

Inside, all was cobwebby and dim. Paddy, peering,

could make out an oil drum laid on its side in a sand-filled crib, with a stovepipe poking from it to vanish through a metal sheet in the roof. At least, they'd have a stove of sorts.

On the other side of the shack's single narrow room were two pole bunks, one above the other, in which withered boughs that had once been evergreen had been heaped for mattresses. It was years since those bunks had been slept in. The boughs were reduced to firetraps.

A split-log shutter had been spiked over the single window let into the front of the shack. With the axe from their outfit, which he had prudently brought up from the canoe with him, Mayus pried the shutter loose.

The window lacked glass. Sunlight streamed in through the rectangle to reveal a crude cedar-slab floor. Paddy saw that the sun also filtered through the cedar-shake roof by way of numerous gaps where shakes had been ripped off by winter's howling gales.

"Sure ain't much of a layout," Mayus remarked. He sounded really low in his spirits; obviously, his uneasiness about staying on Diablo Island still rode him.

"Could be worse," Paddy said with determined cheerfulness. The place was no palace, but at least it did have walls, a floor and an apology for a roof. It could be made liveable. "When we get it patched up and the roof mended," he said to Mayus, "it'll do fine."

One item they'd overlooked in their outfitting was a broom. Mayus, calling on his Kwakiutl handcraft, put together a serviceable sweeper out of twigs of the golden-flowering broom that rioted on the slopes. These he lashed to a handle hacked from an ocean-spray clump. With a good sweep-out, the shack began to look more habitable. While Paddy swept, Mayus emptied the bunks of their dried-up mattresses, which he hauled outside for later burning.

Paddy nodded toward the woods. "How'd you like to get us fresh mattress stuff?" he asked.

But Mayus, usually quick to undertake a job, shook his head. "I'll let you look after that," he said. "Me, I'll get busy on the roof."

Cutting hemlock boughs with their lacy green sprays in the timber fringe, Paddy could hear Mayus pounding replacement shakes into their roof. He piled his take of branches on his axe handle as he remembered being taught to do on a wild-country camping trip, and jogged back down-slope with his load to lay their new mattresses. Then he gave Mayus a hand, spotting gaps from below while Mayus attended to the roof-patching. When they needed more shakes, they liberated them from the sagging roofs of other shanties.

Next, working together, they fitted new driftwood legs to an old table top which they found bleaching amid a tangle of blackberry vines.

"You know," Paddy said, with a grin for Mayus, "we're doing okay!"

"Yeah," Mayus said. But he was far from the cheerful racoon to which he owed his Kwakiutl name, and it was plain from his tone that he wished himself elsewhere.

Paddy left it at that. He didn't know what ailed Mayus, and it worried him. But they had a home to finish setting up, and he'd best get on with it. Axe swinging from his fist, he ventured on along the line of ancient handliners' shacks.

Well down the straggling row of toppled sides and tumbled roofs, he made a useful find. In a collapsed front wall he came on a window entire and complete. Working with finicky care, Paddy pried the window frame loose from the wall. Then, carrying it gingerly, he headed back to the home shanty.

Glory be! Here was a triumph! The frame with its

precious glass fitted so exactly into the gaping rectangle in their own front wall that no more than a little cautious toe-nailing was needed to secure it. As a final touch, Mayus cut a makeshift door hinge from the top of an old gumboot exhumed from under the bunks. He nailed it in place. The door swung easily, and a dab of bacon grease from their stores took the squeal out of the surviving metal hinge.

That done, Mayus set about rigging a sturdy bar, and a pair of wooden brackets to secure their door. Finished, he dropped the bar in place across the brackets and gave the door a testing pull.

Paddy, curious, watched the performance. It seemed to him that the last thing they needed on little, deserted Diablo Island was a lock for their door. But if it would make Mayus happier, so be it!

6

A Live and Kicking Ghost

Even though the afternoon was well along toward evening, the shack remained achingly hot. The prospect of firing up the oil-drum stove and cooking a meal indoors had no appeal whatever. Paddy and Mayus toted stones up from the beach to make themselves an outdoor fireplace. For fuel, they beavered together an enormous pile of drift-cedar chunks, resiny fir knots and slabs of Douglas fir bark shed by log booms heading down-straits in tow behind powerful tugboats.

Mayus shaved fragrant red cedar peelings from a driftwood stick. These he arranged in a little pyramid. Then he raised his black head from his work and asked Paddy, "How about a match?"

Paddy searched his pockets. No matches. He started for his skiff. Then he remembered: their match supply had taken a ruinous dunking.

"I'm out of matches," he said. "Better use one of yours."

"That's why I asked you, for Pete's sake," Mayus told him. "I haven't got any."

They gazed at each other in dismay. Then a slow grin quirked Mayus' face.

"More'n one way to skin a cat," he said. He got up off his heels and went into the shack, to emerge with a most curious bag in his hands. The bag was fashioned of some crinkly grey material that Paddy couldn't identify.

"What's that?" he asked.

"Dunno what you'd call it in white people's lingo," Mayus said, fingers busy with the thong that secured the bag. "Medicine sack, maybe. Anyhow, my gram, she holds by the old ways. She made me bring it along." He added, "It's made of salmon skin."

Mayus delved a hand into the sack. He fetched out a large, heart-shaped cockle shell, its matched and fluted halves tied together with a wrapping of wiry twine.

Paddy, bump of curiosity prickling, watched Mayus untie the twine. Carefully, he lifted the top half of the shell. Both halves were stuffed with what looked to be punk of the sort one finds in a rotted tree stump.

"What's that rig?" Paddy asked.

"Fire starter." Mayus gave Paddy a quick grin. "In olden days, my people carried 'em on long canoe trips. There's a live coal in the punk. It just sits there and smoulders 'till it's needed."

Hunkered down again, Mayus reached behind him for a handful of dried grass. Cautiously, holding the lower half of his shell close to his face, he began to blow. A tiny wisp of smoke coiled from the shell. It grew stronger. A red spot glowed in the punk. Mayus set his clump of brown grass against the punk: it too began to smoke.

Smiling, Mayus waved the grass wad to and fro. Sudden flame burst from it. Mayus tucked the burning grass under his pyramid of cedar shavings, which caught hold with a briskly reassuring snap-and-crack. Mayus added heavier fuel. He was rewarded with a dance of flames.

"Those old ones," he said, still with the smile lightening his face, "they was smart. Knew all kinds of tricks."

Carefully, he tied the halves of his fire-maker together and returned it to the sack.

It had been an impressive demonstration. Also — and for this, Paddy was grateful — it had taken Mayus's mind off his secret worries for at least a few minutes.

When their fire had burned to coals, Paddy set their big black frying pan across a pair of rocks, and dabbed a nut of bear lard into its bottom to grease it.

"Bear steaks okay with you?" he asked Mayus. "It's off a young one, never got around to eating fish, so it tastes okay."

Mayus shook his head. "Bear's out for me," he said. "I'm not allowed to eat bear meat."

"Another of those Indian things?" Paddy asked, trying not to grin.

"Yeah. If I eat bear, I won't catch any salmon. First bear laid it on my people a long time ago. Taught 'em how to fish."

"Then you'd better fry up some ham," Paddy said. "Unless you can't eat that, either."

"Ham's fine," said Mayus. "The salmon people got nothing against ham." He reached for his belt-knife and began to carve himself a generous portion of Grandfather Logan's hard-cured ham.

While Paddy's bear steak sizzled in the pan, he squatted by the fire with a feeling of deep content upon him. He was never happier than when out like this, living rough in lonely country. He guessed it had been the same with his Canadian-born dad, whom cities had always bothered, and who had died in a rock slide while following his profession as a field geologist in Alaska.

Paddy flipped his steak over. The heat of the afternoon was beginning to drain away at last; a cool little breath of air wandered from the woods behind the shack to finger his face.

Mayus frizzled his section of ham. They ate hungrily, sitting cross-legged by the fire with their tin plates in their laps.

"Tomorrow we'll have to start right in fishing," Paddy said, and Mayus answered him, "Yeah...yeah, I guess so."

Paddy glanced at Mayus with a return of his worry. Mayus's dark mood continued to puzzle him. He seemed to be tense, constantly on edge, as if he were listening for someone or something. But best pay no attention to it, Paddy decided. Give him time to get used to the island and Mayus would shake off the fit.

Paddy got up with his empty plate in his hand. "Let's go hunt for that spring," he suggested. "We'll be needing water."

Mayus climbed to his feet in silence. He followed Paddy back from the foreshore through the long wild grass toward the woods.

They mounted to the crest of a rock outcropping. At the edge of a tongue of evergreens, directly ahead of them, loomed the cedar-plank silhouette of the killer whale in the claws of the thunderbird. It had been startling when seen from the water. Here at close range, a lurid sunset edging it with fire, it was awesome. Seen close up like this, it was plain that the paint which still clung to the wood in vestigial traces had been applied a long time in the past.

"Hey," Paddy said softly. "Isn't that something!"

Mayus didn't answer. Paddy shot a side-glance at his companion. The Kwakiutl boy stood as if frozen, eyes wide, staring at the monstrous figures.

"What's wrong?" Paddy demanded. "You'd better tell me."

"That's what's wrong." Mayus spoke in a strained undertone, gaze still on Killer Whale and Thunderbird. "That's what they call a mortuary figure. It's the same as a tombstone." He took a deep breath to steady himself. "I didn't know it when we came over, but this island's one of the old people's burying places. They put 'em in boxes up in the trees..."

Mayus broke off abruptly. He turned away. "I'm gettin' out of here. This place is spooked."

"Aw, don't be silly!" Paddy laid a restraining hand on Mayus' arm. "Nothing's going to hurt us. All that was in the old times." He forced a laugh, displaying more assurance than he felt. "I'll bet there's not even old bones left."

Mayus shrugged Paddy's hand off. He spoke with determination. "Well, I don't figure on finding out." Hurrying, Mayus started back in the direction of their shanty.

Paddy watched Mayus go. The evening was suddenly lonely without him, the silence pressing in. Just the same, if they were to stay here on Diablo—and he was by no means sure he could persuade Mayus to stay—they'd need to find fresh water.

After a good deal of searching, Paddy stumbled on the spring. It nestled cupped at the bottom of a steep and fern-hung cleft. He jolted down between crowding tree trunks, attracted by the gleam of water, and dropped to his knees beside the miniature basin. Parting black-stemmed ferns, he dipped a hand and raised it dripping to his mouth. The water was icy and clear as air.

That, at least, was one problem solved. Paddy sank his first lard pail, taking care not to stir up the basin. When that was full he lifted it clear and filled his second pail to the brim.

He felt good again. Finding the spring had caused the shadows to lift. With the spring to draw on, they could stay on Diablo as long as they wanted...

Mayus's voice, raised in an urgent yell, sent the thought skittering. Looking down-slope, he saw Mayus tearing across the foreshore to the beach. Beyond him, black against the evening quicksilver of the lagoon, the skiff and the canoe drifted toward the entrance in the grip of the ebb-tide.

But that couldn't be! They'd left both boats hauled up well beyond the tide's highest range.

Paddy set his pails down. He galloped through the long grass for the beach, leaping down to the first of the serried ranks of driftlogs as Mayus splashed into the lagoon.

Mayus waded until he was armpit deep, then swam with powerful strokes, forging his way out to the canoe. Arrived, he tipped the gunwale down, propelled himself inboard with a dexterous heave-and-roll, and reached for his oars.

Mayus recovered Paddy's skiff, knotted its painter around in a canoe thwart and pulled for the beach with the skiff bobbing and weaving in his wake.

Dripping, he climbed out as the canoe stem touched the pebbles.

"We can't have pulled 'em up far enough," Paddy said, not believing it. "We'll know better next time."

"Wasn't that," Mayus said. He stood dark and brooding, a faded red bandana tied as a headband around his long black hair. His face was shadowed, as if he had withdrawn into some wilder past. "Someone . . . something turned those boats loose. We're not wanted here. We better get off."

Paddy realized with a sinking feeling that their venture could end before it was well began.

"Listen," he said, "I still think it was that old sneak tide." He forced a smile. "We're both pretty jumpy right now. S'pose we wait till morning, then talk it over?"

Mayus didn't reply. He turned abruptly away, and hurried up toward the shack. Paddy stood for a moment looking after Mayus. Then, walking slowly, he brushed through the knee-high downland grass to where he had left his water pails.

When he returned to the shack, the door was barred.

"Just me," he called. "Open up!"

He heard the rattle of the bar as Mayus lifted it from its brackets. Mayus's face, when he opened the door, was carefully blank . . . so wooden that Paddy swallowed back words he'd meant to drop. He had intended to kid Mayus, try to jolly him out of his dark mood. But it occurred to Paddy, as he set his pails among the nettles that grew thick under their window that right now, silence might be worth any amount of chatter.

The two-mile row from Bukwis and the labour of fixing up the shack had wearied them. Even before full dark had moved in, Paddy found himself yawning fit to un-hinge his jaws.

"Guess I'll turn in," he said.

"Me too," Mayus said. He crossed the door and care-fully placed the wooden bar in the brackets. The hem-lock-frond mattress proved to be miserably inadequate. Paddy, shifting about in an attempt to find a comfortable position, told himself he should have remembered what a lot of browse was needed for a decent bed, and cut twice as much more. Tomorrow, he vowed as he settled his hipbone against the unyielding poles of his bunk, they'd certainly take care of that. *Always provided*, the bleak thought hit him, *that we're still here tomorrow . . .*

Mayus had climbed into the upper bunk. He lay per-fectly still, but Paddy sensed that he hadn't gone to sleep.

"How you doing up there?" he called.

"Fine," Mayus answered him. "I'm doin' fine." But his tone wasn't convincing.

The warmth of his blankets was comforting to Paddy. The poles under his skimpy mattress of hemlock feathers bothered him less. He drifted off into a dream in which he was tooling his new bike along Birch Street, skimming folded newspapers on to subscribers' porches.

He was level with old Mrs. Lazenby's house, and lining up on her porch with special care, when a whisper from overhead bored through to him.

"Paddy... You awake?"

He jolted out of his dream. "Yeah," he whispered. "What's up?"

Back came the tense whisper. "Somethin's out there. Listen!"

Paddy listened, lips parted to hear the better. He listened so hard that he could hear the blood singing in his ears.

Then, just as he was about to give Mayus a reassuring, "You're nuts!" he heard it.

A brushing and slithering. A scratching at their door. Then, in a muffled and eerie quaver, a voice that caused the hair to prickle on the back of his neck.

"*Oh... Oh... Oh...*" the voice wailed.

In the bunk above, Mayus lay deathly still. Rigid as a board, Paddy waited, while the chills chased each other up and down his spine.

The voice reached for them again. "We are the spirits of the dead ones." The voice climbed to a whine. "You disturb our sleep. Go and don't ever come back!"

Then, to make terror complete, a dim white shape wavered across the window pane.

"It's a ghost." Mayus's voice came down to Paddy in a reedy squeak. "What'll we do?"

Sounds of a sudden commotion reached them from outside. Paddy heard a thud and a thumping, then the clatter of tinware.

From the other side of the barred door, a voice...a girl's voice...came out with an unghostly "Damn!"

Paddy rolled out of his bunk. "That's no spook!" he snapped at Mayus as he groped in his rucksack for his flashlight. "I know who that is..."

Behind him, he heard Mayus clambering from his own bunk. He grabbed the bar, lifted it from its brackets, and kicked the door open. The beam of his flash caught and pinned Lynn Hutchins. Draped in a white sheet, she scrabbled among the nettles under the window on her hands and knees. A foot was jammed in one of Paddy's water pails. From the gloom beyond Lynn, Paddy's eye caught movement, a mere vanishing flicker.

"All right." Paddy advanced through the doorway, scowling, gripping the bar like a club. "What're you doing, sneaking around here?"

Lynn, sitting now, tugged with both hands at the pail that had trapped her foot. She was spitting mad: the glare she gave Paddy would fry an egg.

"You've got no right here," she burst out. "This is my place, I've been here for years! Then you come over and move in and start ruckusing and helling around...!"

"Like heck it's your place," Mayus said sharply. "This island, all these islands are Indian land. They belong to my people."

"Well, I've got squatter's rights," Lynn snapped. She worked the pail loose, scrambled to her feet, and hurled the pail violently into the night.

"We're here," Paddy said to her, "and we're going to stay." He dropped the bar and turned to Mayus. His question was also a challenge.

"That's right, isn't it?"

"It sure is," Mayus agreed sturdily. "Here we are an' here we stay, an' you better shove off."

"I will. Don't worry about that." Lynn's tone was venom-

ous. "Only I'll tell you one thing first. Handlining isn't for greenhorns. You'll starve. And believe me, I hope you do!"

Paddy considered her, fighting a grin. "Aw, come on," he said. "This is crazy. We're here together, so why don't we be friends?"

The words sparked Lynn to deeper anger. She stared at him, coppery hair around her face, eyes flashing.

"Friends!" she repeated. Then, in icy tones, "I don't need friends."

She turned abruptly and plunged into the dark of the moonless night, trailing her bedsheet.

Mayus called a question after her: "Hey, Lynn! Was it you who turned our boats loose?"

But he got no answer.

Paddy let out his breath in a long sigh. They grinned at each other.

"Oh boy!" Mayus said. "That scared me out of a year's growth."

"Me too," Paddy said. He looked at Mayus, and what he saw — a return of the old cockiness — caused his heart to lift.

"How are you doing?" he asked.

"Me?" Mayus said. "I'm okay. Guess I got all the scaredness out of my system." A slow grin lightened his face. "No sweat! We'll handline in spite of Lynn Hutchins. An' we'll catch fish."

"I sure hope so," Paddy said soberly. Now that their gamble had been taken, he was less confident than he'd been when they laid their plans on Bukwis Island.

The sea was big, and they were very small. It occurred to Paddy also that what he didn't know about rowboat fishing for salmon would fill a large book.

"You know," Mayus said, "I've gone an' worked up an appetite. I keep thinkin' about that ham."

They went back into the shanty. And this time, Paddy noticed, Mayus didn't bother to bar the door.

But even though Mayus had got his spunk back, Paddy decided it might be smarter to wait until daylight to tell Mayus that Lynn Hutchins hadn't come ghost knocking alone. Just for an instant when he'd opened the door, he had glimpsed another figure — blurred, indistinct and blending with the darkness — that watched from the shadows.

7

To Catch a Silver Salmon

Tired to the bone, they slept until the heat of the morning sun on the low roof threatened to parboil them.

Paddy rolled out, yawning and rubbing his eyes, to find Mayus already up. A fire popped and crackled in their outdoor hearth. Mayus had four brown eggs that had survived the swamping ranged in a row on a cedar slab, and ham sputtered in the frying pan.

"Hope you're hungry," he said, poking vigorously at the ham with a fork lashed to an ocean-spray sapling. "We got a big day coming up."

Paddy reached to a tin plate propped on a couple of stones for a piece of only slightly singed toast. "Where do we fish?" he asked.

"Oh . . . out there." With a sweep of his arm, Mayus covered the channel that sparkled between Diablo and Little Diablo, also the archipelago of lesser islets and reefs that peppered the sea beyond. "She's all good salmon water."

"There sure is a lot of it," Paddy remarked dubiously.

It occurred to him that Mayus didn't seem to know much about handlining either.

Breakfast over, dishes washed, they turned to their tackle . . . and once again, their fluky luck turned against them.

"Where's the line?" Mayus called over his shoulder, digging like a woodchuck in their higgledy-piggledy pile of gear. "Can't find it anywhere."

"Last I saw," Paddy said, "it was right in the bag with our other tackle."

"Well it isn't now," Mayus said.

Paddy joined Mayus in the search. But the line had gone — vanished — and finally the unpalatable truth dawned on them.

"When I swamped," Paddy said. "I'll bet it went overside."

"Well," Mayus said grimly, "there goes our fishing."

"It could have drifted in on the tide." Paddy said, without much hope. "A big hank like that. It'd float."

But though they combed the lagoon shore and scrambled over the confining rock points to search the open beach, they failed to turn up the bundle of line on which their fishing depended.

"We'll have to row back and buy more," Paddy said. "We're out of money but Mrs. Busby will put it on the books." He added glumly, "I lost it, so I'll row over."

"Hold up," Mayus told him. He picked up his salmon-skin medicine bag and loosed the drawstring at its throat. Groping in its depths, he fetched out a ball of rough grey twine the size of his two fists.

"Kwakiutl fishline," he said. "The old people made it out of nettle fibre. My gram stuck it in."

"Doesn't look like it would hold a salmon," Paddy said.

"No?" Mayus gave him a superior grin. "Well, let's see you break it!"

He tossed the ball to Paddy, who unwound a two-foot length and took a wrap around each hand. Then he hauled, applying more pressure and still more, until the nettle-fibre line of the elder Kwakiutl threatened to cut into his fingers.

Paddy looked at the line with new respect. "Tough stuff," he said. "Those old people knew what they were doing."

The ball of nettle-fibre twine gave them a handline each, to be wound on cedarwood holders. Then they split the rest of the gear . . . piano-wire leaders, spoons of various sizes and finishes, and sinkers in weights from two ounces to a pound.

Paddy stowed his equipment in the outer pocket of his rucksack, and slid his new spruce oars from the porch roof where he'd stashed them the previous evening.

Together, they trudged down to the beach. They gave each other a hand with the boat-launching: first they slid Mayus's black dugout off its driftlogs and into the lagoon shallows, then crunched back for Paddy's heavier, clumsier skiff.

Floating boat-by-boat, they exchanged grins.

"Well . . ." Paddy said.

"Here goes nothing!" Mayus said.

They dipped oars and eased out toward a lagoon entrance through which mountainous cresters no longer surged. The gut lay flat and unrippled: the sea beyond glittered as if its lightly-ruffled surface had been sprinkled with diamonds: no whitecaps showed. It was a fair day. And maybe, Paddy thought with a quickening of excitement, it would be a lucky day!

Well clear of the entrance gut, he slid his oars inboard. With the sun roasting his shoulders through his shirt, he bent over his gear. He chose a spoon—a slim silver wabbler about four inches long—and clipped it to a leader. The spoon, twinkling alongside his boat, looked minnow-like and enticing. A salmon would find that mouthful hard to refuse.

Paddy secured an eight-ounce sinker to his line a few feet above the leader, then, between strokes on his oars, paid out nettle-fibre until the lure fished at mid-depth about seventy feet astern.

He was in business — on the salmon grounds and fishing. All that now remained was for the salmon, those silvery money-fish, to co-operate! Paddy slipknotted the line around his left leg below the knee, then settled to his rowing.

The new spruce oars his grandfather had made for him were a treat to use. They entered the water cleanly and lifted out smoothly. Paddy felt that he could row forever, if need be. He glanced out to see Mayus easing along on parallel course a quarter-mile away. The sun was warm, the sea gentle, the steady pulsing of the gear telegraphed itself up the line to his leg. It was a good day, a great day to be alive . . .

A sudden tightening of the line caused him to clatter his oars inboard. He snatched his leg-knot free and began to haul. But it wasn't a fish; he had merely shaved too close to one of the trailing kelp beds and fouled his rigging.

For a hot, sweaty quarter of an hour, Paddy laboured to free his hook from its grip in a deep-down kelp stem. Then, when he finally succeeded in wrenching free, his line surfaced with leader trailing limp behind it. His spoon was gone.

Scowling, Paddy rummaged a new spoon from his rucksack and bent it on to his leader. Not so good a start. But he'd hold farther out from the treacherous kelp beds next time.

Off the tapering snout of Little Diablo, his line tugged again. No kelp this time, but a live and active fish. Paddy shipped oars and, with an exultant yell to Mayus, began to pulley-haul line aboard.

Leaning overside, he strained his eyes for a glimpse of the fish. Then he saw it, a lean brown shadow that twirled deep down. The creature showed a white belly. Even to Paddy's hopeful vision, it somehow didn't look like a salmon.

He gripped the leader by the swivel at its top end, and lifted. The fish's head broke water. Paddy gaped at the triangular snout, the wicked green eyes, and the mean mouth set under the jaw. He had caught a shark — a little shark — a dogfish easily three feet long.

A dark tail-lobe broke the surface. As Paddy hoisted the dogfish higher, the tail gave a sudden lash. Pain stabbed at the base of one thumb. A drop of blood appeared.

Mayus was hailing him. "Hi... What you got?"

"Dogfish," Paddy called back.

"Be careful with him," Mayus hollered. "They got a thorn down near their tail. If it jags you, it'll fester."

Now he tells me! Paddy whacked the dogfish on its snout with his fish club. Avoiding the snapping jaws with their razor teeth, he immobilized the writhing brute with his gaff while he worked his hook free. Disgusted, he watched the dogfish shadow off into the depths.

Paddy dabbled his hand overside. The saltwater eased the stinging.

"Catch any?" he called to Mayus, whose canoe now rode only a hundred feet distant.

The answer came back. "Not yet. I'm goin' try the other side of Little Diablo."

In this big water, it was better if they fished in convoy. Paddy, his line in business once more, jogged off after Mayus's easy-gliding canoe. The sun and the warm breath of breeze soothed his ruffled feelings. It was good to be out like this, free and alone on the blue water, with always the chance of a salmon to intercept the lure that sparkled deep below . . .

As if in response to the thought, the line tightened around his leg in a hard, sustained pull.

Paddy slithered his oars in back of him and reached for the line. Whatever was down there, yanking and tugging, it was no dogfish! Not this time. It had weight and power. It undulated off through the water, fighting deep, while Paddy yielded line grudgingly from the coils on the skiff's bottomboards.

A glance told him there was very little of the nettle-fibre line left. He locked his fists around the cord, trying to check the fish's savage lunges. The skiff moved on, in tow, with a sustained rustle of parted water under its bows.

Mayus had hauled in his own line. The canoe rode close alongside.

"What you got there, anyhow?" he called.

"Don't know." Paddy, breathless from the strain, tightened his grip, leaned back on the line, and recovered a yard.

He was standing now, braced solidly. He could feel the weight and power of his fish as it battled for its freedom. It came to him that he might have hooked a tyee salmon — one of those super-large Chinooks that sometimes cruised these waters on the way to their spawning grounds. A fighter that would measure four feet or more from nose to tail, and that would weigh forty . . . sixty . . . seventy pounds or better.

Movement flickered in the corner of his eye. Another boat had eased into his cone of vision; a slim green carvel. Paddy glimpsed Lynn Hutchins' coppery helmet of close-cropped hair.

Well, let her watch! Maybe when she saw him boat his tyee, she'd think better of their chances of making a stake.

Paddy flicked a glance to the boat bottom. His club and gaff lay handy: soon, now, he'd be needing them. He set his heels and hauled again. The fish had stopped its struggling. It came up a dead weight.

Through the clear water, Paddy saw a wide white gleam. Whatever he'd hooked appeared to be kite-shaped, and was broad as a door. Not a salmon—he'd guessed wrong there—but what the devil was the beast?

Its head parted the surface. Paddy stared at the enormous fish, which lay with dark brown back awash. He reached for his gaff.

In a vague, preoccupied way, he was aware that Mayus was shouting at him.

"Club it! Don't gaff it! Don't haul it in your boat!"

Nuts! He wanted it in his boat. Paddy snatched up his gaff, slipped its shepherd's-crook steel hook under one of the fish's massive gill plates, and heaved.

Straining mightily, he lifted half of the monster's flat, broad length above the surface. Another heave skidded it over the gunwale and into his skiff.

On the instant, all hell broke loose.

The wide tail lashed. The head rose and slammed down on the bottomboards with a crash that threatened to stave in the planking. Paddy's gaff spun overboard in a high arc. Caught by the madly lashing tail, his bag of fishing gear followed.

This fish, this demon creature with the goggling eyes set close together on top of its head, was bouncing all over his boat.

Another sweep of its tail scythed his ankles from under him. He toppled backward over the rowing thwart to sprawl with a thump that knocked the wind out of him. The back of his head connected with the bow seat, sending light flashes and zigzags through his spinning brain. He was dimly aware of a splash, and from Mayus, a wild yell. Then he was alone in his rocking skiff, with one oar and his gaff-hook bobbing away on the ripples. His broken handline trailed over the side.

Laughter — a girl's laughter — got through to him. Lynn sat in her rowboat, laughing fit to kill, with head thrown back and not a trace of sympathy on her face.

Of his fish, there was no sign.

Mayus recovered Paddy's oar and gaff. His face was peculiarly wooden.

"Well," Paddy demanded, "Why aren't you laughing too?"

"Us Kwakiutl aren't like that," Mayus told him. "We don't laugh at someone else's troubles."

Scowling, Paddy fitted the oar into its rowlock and began to stroke. As he pulled away, he heard a sound like the complaining of a rusty hinge. Mayus, doubled over his knees with shoulders shaking and eyes squinched up, was laughing his head off.

"Okay," Paddy called grumpily. "Now you've had your fun, what was it?"

"Ol' Woman of the Sea," Mayus told him. "What you call halibut." His lips trembled, but by a stern effort he held the grin back. "Listen, next time you hook a real big halibut, for cat's sake, don't yank it inboard while it's still green. Club it first. . . take the spunk outa it!"

Lynn's boat ghosted past on Paddy's other side. The girl flipped a mocking hand at him. Her cedarwood-coloured hair shone in the sunlight, and on her face the Cheshire-cat smile lingered. She dipped her oars and the smooth-hulled rowboat eased away. But not before Paddy caught the glint of silver on its bottom stretcher. Salmon! To add insult to injury, Lynn had outfished him.

Dispiritedly, Paddy took stock of his situation. Much of his fishing tackle had taken the deep six: he had only two spoons left, plus a half-pound weight and a scatteration of hooks and swivels.

"I'll have to go in to camp," he told Mayus. "All right if I use the rest of that nettle-fibre line of yours?"

"Sure," Mayus said. "How 'bout if you bring us out a ham sam'wich an' some water? I'm starving."

"You're always starving," Paddy said. Then as a thought struck him, "Would that fish, that halibut, have been worth anything?"

"It was a real big one," Mayus said. He did some mental figuring, then announced cheerfully, "Be worth about ten, fifteen bucks."

With that knife to twist in the wound, Paddy put his skiff through the lagoon entrance. His palms, still blistered from the day before, had begun to hurt again, and the place where the dogfish had jagged him itched and burned. His first fishing day hadn't exactly been a howling success.

As he pulled for the beach, he saw that the slender green rowboat had put in before him, its lines so gracefully sea-kind that they made Paddy's tar-splotched skiff look like a cabbage crate.

Watched from a rock by a bald eagle, and with a nimbus of white-winged seagulls planing above her, Lynn hunkered at the edge of the lagoon beside her boat. She was gutting fish. Paddy, stabbed by envy, frowned at the spectacle as he hopped overside and guided his boat's nose to the shingle.

That nuisancy girl didn't have just one salmon, or two, but a whole mess of them!

Lynn reached for yet another fish from her catch. It was long, broad and silvery — a fine salmon, a money-fish. She waggled it tauntingly in Paddy's direction.

Paddy ignored her. With vicious lunges, he hauled the skiff clear of the tide. Then, still elaborately disregarding Lynn where she knelt with knife in fist, Paddy marched up the beach toward the shack. He'd patch up his tackle and shove off again. There were salmon to be caught out yonder—Lynn had demonstrated that—and when he got the hang of it, he'd show her a thing or two!

He wasn't hungry himself. Too darn mad. But he fixed a hefty sandwich for Mayus, and filled a couple of pop bottles with spring water.

They fished until late afternoon. In the last moments, as they were preparing to knock off for the day, Mayus did hook and land one runty little salmon.

"A pink," Mayus said as he unhooked it. "What we call a humpback." He added morosely, "Heck, it ain't worth rowing over to the cannery with."

They plodded home across mirror-calm water in which a painted sunset was reflected. As they landed, they saw Lynn's rowboat, a sliver of green, overturned across drift-logs well along the beach. A thin coil of smoke rose from the other side of the rock point to the north. She must occupy a shack up that way.

Paddy muttered to Mayus as they climbed stiffly over the logs, "You know how many she caught? Eight salmon."

"Coho or springs or pinks?" Mayus asked; and Paddy answered him with a grumpy, "How would I know?"

"That's the trouble," Mayus said. "We should know." He paused, oars across his shoulder. "We ought to know all kinds of things that we don't."

"We'll learn," Paddy told him without much conviction. "You wait and see. We'll show 'em tomorrow!"

8

A Call For Help

Mayus, who had slipped into the role of camp cook, fixed his salmon Indian-style for their dinner. First, with his thin-bladed fish knife, he split it down the back, opening it into a snowshoe-shaped slab of red meat. Next, with delicate strokes of his knife, he cut away the spine with its sturdy lateral bones attached like the branches of a tree. Paddy, watching, saw that Mayus set the backbone along with head, fins and guts carefully aside on a fragment of drift-plank.

From the foreshore scrub, Mayus next trimmed a sturdy ocean-spray sapling. He split the sapling for two-thirds of its length with their axe. Then he inserted the salmon into the cleft, securing it and spreading it wide open with splints of beach cedar which he pushed crosswise at spaced intervals through the split.

Finally, Mayus rammed the thick end of his sapling into the pebbles at the edge of their hearth, and supported it with piled stones so that the salmon leaned flesh-side down toward their fire.

In a surprisingly short time, the fish began to sizzle and to drip its rich juices. By degrees, its meat changed colour from red to a succulent golden-brown. Mayus gave it a testing prod with his knife-point. Then, frowning judiciously, he added a couple more chunks of split alderwood to the fire.

The combined aroma of alder smoke and broiling salmon set Paddy's mouth watering.

"Smells good," he said, eyeing their dinner wolfishly.

"It'll taste better," Mayus assured him.

When the salmon skin had changed colour to a rich mahogany, and the slab no longer dripped its fat on to the coals, Mayus reversed his sapling frame to expose the other side to the heat.

"Not long now," he said. "You better lay out the plates."

Paddy set their table: four salvaged planks laid across a pair of handy driftlogs. He hacked thick slices from a loaf, noting with mild dismay that it was the last of three they'd brought from the cannery.

With a flourish, Mayus yanked his salmon-laden sapling from its supporting nest of rocks. He fetched it to the table, where he laid it proudly on the planks. With hand wrapped in a gunny sack, he freed the smoking oval of fish from sapling and splints.

"First I ever cooked," he said. "My gram'ma showed me how. Come an' get it!"

Paddy needed no second dinner call. He grabbed knife and fork and loaded his tin plate.

In the past, he had regarded fish dubiously, as second-rate food. But never had he tasted anything so good! The salmon, crisp brown on the outside and steaming pink within, had acquired a unique flavour that a dash from Mayus's precious oolichan oil jug heightened. It needed neither pepper nor salt. The underlying trace of smoke, the oil and its own natural tang were spices enough.

"S'good," Paddy told Mayus through a mouthful. "Real good!"

Not even the sight of Lynn Hutchins rowing past on her way to the cannery with her pay-load could take the edge off that meal. They ate hugely—ate until they could hold no more—then built up the fire and finished off with mugs of heavily-sugared tea.

Reluctantly at last, Paddy upsprung his shoulders from the log against which he had been reclining. He got to his feet.

"You did the cooking," He said. "Fair's fair. I'll clean up."

So full that he had to do everything in slow motion, Paddy fetched water from the spring and set it over the fire to heat. He stacked plates and cups, collected random scraps from the table and consigned them to the fire.

His dishwater heated fast. He lifted off the steaming pail, renewed the fire with chunks of cedar which sent the flames spiring briskly into the dusk, then upended the salmon backbone, head and oddments into the blaze.

Mayus, chin sunk on chest, sprawled fast asleep. Paddy spared him a grin as he sluiced hot water on their plates. Overhead, the first star showed in an apple-green evening sky.

"Starlight, star bright . . ." Paddy wished on the star. He wished for luck in their fishing.

When the dishes were squared away, he poked Mayus into life with a runner toe.

"Boy," he said, grinning over Mayus, "are you ever the old dormouse! Wake up and go to bed."

Mayus sat up. He sniffed. Then he scrambled to his feet.

"Where's those salmon trimmings?" he demanded."

"I burned 'em," Paddy answered. Then, puzzled, "Why? What's wrong?

"Well," Mayus said, eyeing him darkly, "you sure fixed us proper. We should have put the head an' the backbone an' all back in the sea, so's the rest of the salmon would know we respected them, and treat us right."

"That's another of your Indian things, huh?" Paddy was unimpressed.

"Yeah," said Mayus, biting off his words. "It's an Iny'an thing. Pretty important thing, too."

Mayus turned abruptly from the fire. He plodded off toward the shack, hands jammed in pockets and head down.

Only a little worried, Paddy watched him go. Okay, so he'd broken one of Mayus's cockeyed Kwakiutl rules! But could anything like that hurt their fishing chances?

They caught no salmon next day, or the day after that, nor on any day of the week that followed.

It was not for lack of trying. They rolled out early, hit the salmon grounds immediately after breakfast, and with only time out for a brief lunch-break afloat, kept their lines in the water until late afternoon.

The rowing blisters on Paddy's hands — and the companion raw circles on his butt from constant rubbing on the rowing thwart — toughened into callused pads. They took the boats out in sun and rain, and once, recklessly, clung to the grounds in the teeth of a making gale, to thread the needle of the lagoon pass with cresters snapping at their tails to speed them.

The almost-nightly spectacle of Lynn Hutchins rowing past on her way to the cannery with another load of salmon didn't help matters. It merely rubbed salt in the wound; there were salmon on the grounds, perhaps not a big sending, but enough to provide Lynn with a daily catch. But try as they would, Paddy and Mayus couldn't make contact with them.

Meanwhile, their supplies dwindled to the steady attrition of two outsized appetites. Mayus especially proved to be an insatiable eater with no thought of stringing out their provisions.

Late on in their second fishless week, Paddy took stock of their situation.

They were out of coffee and sugar. They had tea still, and a lone can of condensed milk. The smoked salmon and oolichan oil they'd brought from the chief's house were mostly gone, nibbled away by that rat of a Mayus, and the mighty ham from one of Bruce Logan's over-stuffed porkers had been reduced to a nubbin.

We've got dried peas, Paddy reflected as he rummaged in the grub-box for the end of ham. *I'll boil up a bucket of pea soup. The ham'll be just right for it.*

On ham-fortified pea soup, and with the rest of their pilot bread, they'd make out until the fish started biting. . .which surely must be soon!

But Paddy's searching turned up no nubbin of ham. The only trace he could find was a wad of ham-scented cheesecloth in the bottom of the box.

Paddy stared at the limp fragment of cloth. That's what the ham had been wrapped in. He'd stowed it away carefully, himself. The answer was obvious. Mayus had raided the grub supply between meals — helped himself to the last of their ham — guzzled it down without a single thought for the future.

Paddy stood stock-still for a minute. He could feel his cheeks and his ears reddening to the surge of anger that realization of Mayus's unthinking greediness had roused in him. Then, still gripping the cheesecloth, he marched out of the shack and down to the beach where Mayus sat on a log polishing his salmon spoons.

"Hey. . ." Mayus's glance became a stare. His round face lost its smile. "What's buggin' you?"

"This." Paddy flung the cheesecloth at Mayus's feet. "You damn hog! I was saving that ham to make pea soup."

"Mayus set his can of metal polish on the log to one side of him, his salmon spoon on the other. He got to his feet, wooden-faced.

"Okay, so I was hungry. So when us Kwakiutl get hungry, we eat. We don't believe in hoarding."

"Sure," Paddy said, his teeth in the word. "The Indian way!"

The succession of luckless days had shortened Mayus's fuse too. They glared at each other, heads stuck out and fists balled.

"Anyhow, if you hadn't burned those salmon scraps," Mayus charged, "things would a' gone fine."

"That's a lot of crap," Paddy snapped back; and on the instant, Mayus's fist glanced off his cheekbone.

Paddy swung back. His fist connected solidly with Mayus's nose, and he felt the jar of Mayus's knuckles against his mouth. They grappled and rolled in the shingle until they cannoned into a drift log.

The impact broke them apart. They scrambled to their feet, Paddy with a split lip already puffing, and Mayus dripping gore from his nose.

"Now listen," Paddy said, trying to keep the squeak out of his voice, "I'm going to split the food. You keep out of my half, see?"

"You bet I will!" Mayus snapped. "You'd prob'ly charge me for it!"

Paddy had never managed to hold on to a mad for long. He was cooling off already; he had an uneasy feeling that he'd said too much and gone too far. But he was too stubborn to tell Mayus he was sorry.

He strode away, leaving Mayus standing by the log

with his ragged blue bandana pressed to his nose. As his
temper evaporated, he reproached himself bitterly. Mayus was, or had been, his best friend. He'd been silly to
jump him over a nothing thing like a chunk of mouldy
old ham. But the damage was done — Mayus's face had
told him that all too plainly — and he didn't know how to
mend it.

They fixed their own suppers that night with the last
of the potatoes, and fillets from a rock cod jigged out of
a kelp bed. They ate sitting on separate logs. Each did
his own cleaning up. Still not speaking, they climbed into
their bunks. When Paddy got up next morning, Mayus
was already gone. He'd launched his canoe by his lone.
It made a black dot against the blue of open water, far
out from the tip of Little Diablo.

Heavy-hearted, Paddy launched his own boat. He fished all day and into the evening without a strike. Then,
dispiritedly, he pulled back to the lagoon and trudged up
to the shack.

Mayus had already turned in. He huddled under his
blankets, face to the wall, only his roach of stiff black hair
showing. Paddy heated up his portion of leftover potatoes and cod fillets. But he wasn't hungry in spite of his
long day. With his meal only half finished, he slumped
on one of the crates they had beachcombed for seats,
elbows on knees and chin on fists.

He had drifted into a miserable doze when a hard
banging on the door jerked his head up.

A voice, high and urgent, brought him to his feet.

"Open up!" It was Lynn Hutchins. "I need help!"

Paddy yanked the door open. Lynn, breathless and with
eyes like saucers in a white face, stood on the porch. "It's
my granddad," she said. "He's hurt. I need help with him."

Mayus's voice came from overhead. He was sitting up
in his bunk. "What happened to him?"

"He cut his foot with an axe. He's bleeding badly. I've got to get him to the cannery . . . Joe Busby's an industrial first-aid man."

Paddy grabbed for his jacket. He followed Lynn out of the shack. They were running toward the north point when Mayus overtook them. Panting, they toiled up from the beach to the path that led through long, sum-mer-baked grass to Lynn's shanty. The dwelling itself was little more than a burrow gouged into the steep sidehill on which it fronted. Through the years, it had acquired successive layers of driftwood until it humped like a topsy-turvy beehive.

"I didn't know your grandfather lived here," Paddy said to Lynn as he hurried after her.

"There's a lot you don't know," she told him, not turning.

The door resisted her. Paddy set his shoulder to it and heaved. The door slammed back on its hinges. Some-thing spat and hissed from the murky interior. A cat took off from the table in a flying leap. Paddy felt her claws prickling for an instant on his shoulder as she grappled for a purchase, then she was out and away with a parting yowl.

Light flared as Lynn struck a match. She lit a coal-oil lamp. The light increased as she turned up the wick; Paddy saw a man with grey hair and beard lying face-up on a cedar-plank bunk. His left foot was swathed in what looked like a strip torn from a bedsheet. The wrapping was dark with blood, and under his foot, blood had made a pool that soaked through the blankets to drip on the floor.

"We'd better get a tourniquet on that." Paddy dredged into his scout first aid training. "I'll need a strip of cloth and a stick . . . kindling stick will do."

Lynn helping, he looped the cloth below the hurt man's knee, slipped the stick through the loop and began to twist. As the tourniquet tightened, the blood trickle reduced itself to a drip, which presently ceased.

"Can't let that stay on long," Paddy told Lynn. "We'll get him down to your boat."

Lynn's grandfather was not a big man, but he was solidly built, and even though he helped himself as best he could, taking some of his weight on his good foot, it taxed all three of them to shift him down the path and over the driftlogs to where Lynn's boat waited.

For its sixteen-foot length, Lynn's smooth-hulled carvel was surprisingly light. Paddy and Mayus ran it down to the shallows. Then they hustled back to where Lynn knelt in the shingle by her grandfather.

They loaded him on board, settling him on the bottom stretcher with head pillowed on a rolled tarpaulin and feet under the middle thwart.

"I better row," Mayus offered; but Lynn pushed past him to settle herself on the rowing thwart.

"Let me," she said. "I'm used to the boat."

Wedged in the double-ender's sternsheets, the hurt man's head against his ankles and Mayus a dim shape beyond Lynn in the bow, Paddy squinted through blowing rain. He could pick out the lagoon entrance by the ragged line of leaping white on either side of the passage. Rough out there: the waters beyond the pass were all a-prickle with crests rolled up by a wind that increased its velocity each minute.

Before they had left the lagoon a hundred yards astern, the sharp, cycloidal waves that thrust up where wind crashed into tide were assaulting them from every direction. Water slopped inboard.

Lynn, jockeying the boat with head over shoulder, picked her path as best she could among those growling crests. She quartered them into a sea that churned a gout of solid water over the side.

"You better bail!" Mayus shouted to Paddy over the wind's yammering.

Paddy groped under the stern thwart. His fingers closed on a cut down plastic bleach jug, the universal bailer of West Coast smallboat men. He began to scoop water over the side.

They toiled out from under the lee of Diablo Island. The tide ran easier here and the seas were more regular, though still short and appallingly steep. But as Lynn altered course to point the boat's nose for Bukwis Island cannery—no more than a rain-blurred huddle of lights across the angry channel—the cresters altered the nature of their attack.

They began to hump up directly astern in toppling water-hills that kited the rowboat high and rumbled along its sides in a white ruin of foam.

The boat staggered as solid water licked over her quarter. A rogue sea, charging in at an angle, had smashed against her hull.

Paddy plied his bailing can frantically, while he fought to exorcise the panicky thought that flicked into his mind.

Too rough... She won't take much more of this...

He felt a plucking at his leg. A glance at Lynn's grandfather showed that the bearded man's eyes were open in his seamed face. Paddy leaned down to catch his croaked words.

"Tarp. Trail tarp astern..."

Still bailing with one hand, Paddy slipped the rolled tarp from under the hurt man's head. Twisting around, he shook out its folds. The six-by-eight rectangle of heavy canvas streamed in the whipping wind.

The drag as he paid the tarp out astern all but wrenched it from Paddy's hands. Lengths of seine cord were knotted into the corner grommet-holes. Paddy secured the line-lengths through the rub-rails on either side of the rowboat's stern.

Another king-sea roared in from behind them. But the trailing tarpaulin smothered its crest so that it humped under them harmlessly, lifting them high, to slide on past.

Sea-savvy, that trick with the tarp, had eased their passage and just possibly saved their lives.

"Thanks, Mister Hutchins," Paddy said.

The beard cracked in a weak smile. "Y' best call me Ben," he muttered.

Even with Paddy to bail and Mayus to help Lynn con their passage, it remained a nightmare journey. The trailing tarp eased those sharp following seas, but even so, only by fast and continual bailing could Paddy keep the water level down. Once he took time out to ease the tourniquet; he was shocked to note how much water had accumulated during that brief interval. Water was sluicing around his ankles and soaking Ben Hutchins' cocoon of blankets before Lynn surfed them on the wings of a final crest into the quiet and sheltered cannery cove.

Mayus dashed a hand across a forehead that glistened with spray.

"Oh boy," he called to Paddy. "Darn if I know how we made it!"

"We made it because she's real catty with those oars," Paddy said.

Mayus grinned; and with a lightening of his heart, Paddy knew that their quarrel was behind them. Still, he had to say something...to get it off his chest.

"You know," he began, "come to think of it, I'm not all that fussy about pea soup."

Mayus's wet grin widened. "S'pose you go to hell?" he told Paddy amiably.

Lynn cut in on them, cross and worried.

"If you two can spare the time," she snapped, "you might help with my grandfather."

On the cannery float-string, big Joe Busby took over with practised efficiency. He hollered up a couple of hands with a stretcher. They loaded Ben Hutchins on to it, Ben protesting violently that he could make it on one foot, dammit, and packed him up the dock to the first aid lenny which made a cramped annex to the cannery store.

Joe Busby shook his head over the blood-soaked wrappings that bulked like a hornet's nest at the end of Ben's leg. But the axe-slash, a cut so ghastly that Paddy felt his stomach heave as he looked at it, seeped only a little fresh blood.

"No infection," said Joe, busy with sulpha powder and field dressings. "And if that's not a miracle, I don't know what is!"

With Ben Hutchins' foot in clean white bandages, they loaded him on board Gus Sorensen's big white troller, *Westerly*, where she lay snug against a float. Gus, with casual disregard for the weather, had offered to run the hurt man down to hospital at the town of Campbell River across on Vancouver Island. There Ben would receive the further attention his gashed foot demanded.

As he flipped *Westerly*'s stern line loose, Joe Busby squinted at Lynn's carvel tied on at the float.

"Saint Lawrence double-ender," he said. "Ben built her himself. Best smallboat in the world." He flashed the boys a grin as he turned away. "She's the only rowboat would have brought you across on a night like this," he added solemnly.

A hail from the water fetched their heads around. Lynn, her slight body outlined in light, stood in the entrance to *Westerly*'s deckhouse.

"Hey," she called to them. "Thanks! Thanks a lot!"

They watched *Westerly*'s running lights fade in the

murk, then turned to mount the catwalk that pitched steeply from dock to floats.

Weary and wet, but feeling good inside with the knowledge that their breached friendship had been mended, they trampled on up the dock. Joe Busby had offered to put them up for the night at his house and run them back to Diablo in the morning. Right now, they were more than ready for bed.

9

The Raiders

The wind died overnight, leaving only a mild low swell through which Joe Busby's powerful workboat shouldered her way contemptuously as she headed cross-channel for Diablo Island.

Stowed in the waist were cartons of groceries which Mrs. Busby had insisted they load up with. Paddy, lounging beside Joe Busby at the wheel, tried not to think of the long list of new entries in Mrs. Busby's store ledger. Counting what they were already down for, the total in the account book now stood at close to twenty dollars. With the season moving along and no fish showing, the prospect was definitely grim.

Ashore with their plunder on Diablo, they watched the workboat forge out of the lagoon, then packed their supplies up the beach and through the long grass to their shack.

As they neared, Paddy saw that the door stood open. Funny: he was sure he'd closed it. Still, the big wind might have got at it last night, or in their haste he might have left it ajar.

Inside the shack, everything seemed to be just as they'd left it. Even so, Paddy felt a warning prickle along his spine. Everything was the same yet something lingered: the feeling that an alien presence had intruded in their absence.

He began to notice tiny discrepancies. He'd left his rucksack hanging by its shoulder-straps from a peg behind the door. Now it sat on one of the crates that served them as chairs.

Paddy picked up the sack and examined it in detail. Always, he cinched the two short straps that secured the top right down to the last hole in the leather. They had been buckled only midway along each strap. And the draw-cord that fastened the sack was tied with a neat square knot rather than his usual haphazard granny.

Mayus said sharply, "Someone's been in my kit bag." He held up a pair of grey work socks. "I left these done up in a ball. Somebody hauled 'em apart."

"Me too," Paddy said. "Somebody's gone through my stuff."

They traded blank looks. It scared Paddy, gave him a hollow feeling to think that a prowler had raided their camp while they were absent. They had felt completely secure on this barren little island ringed by the sea.

"Some gasboat tramps must a' put in for shelter," Mayus said. With a not quite convincing attempt at casualness, he added, "Don't mean a thing. It happens all the time."

But Paddy wasn't so sure. He remembered Red Dunc Sloan and Arnie Peters with his yellow owl-eyes, and the veiled threat they'd dropped to Gus Sorensen.

"Think it could have been those creek robbers nosing around?" he asked. "You know . . . Arnie and Red Dunc?"

Mayus shrugged. "Could have been anyone. I figure they were lookin' for money."

Paddy snorted. "What a hope!"

Mayus laughed at that, and the shadow lifted. But enough remained to make Paddy resolve to walk carefully and with his weather eye open. Red Dunc and Arnie were bad actors — no men to tangle with.

Life settled once more into its now-familiar routine. Each morning after breakfast — no longer rock cod, thank heaven — they launched the boats for a day of trolling their lures through passages and along island coastlines now familiar to them as the palms of their hands. But though they fished from the string of rocky islets called Dragon Reef on their chart, all the way south to the kelp fringes of Little Diablo, they failed to make a pay-load.

Their jeans and shirts, which last they wore only in the most miserable weather, became ragged and harsh to the feel from exposure to salt air and water. The sun that beat on them most days had tanned Paddy to walnut colour and bleached his brown hair a shade lighter. Even Mayus's skin had taken on a darker tone.

They could row all day without tiring. They were tough and callused, their oars natural extensions of their arms. Also, they had become acutely weather-wise: they held to the fishing grounds through afternoon westerlies that would once have sent them scampering for the shelter of the lagoon. In effect, they had become creatures of the island-studded seas only less so than the gulls and seals, the sooty cormorants and scoter ducks that haunted them.

Once in a while, one or other of them did connect with a salmon. But those incidental catches weren't worth ferrying over to the cannery. Mayus barbecued or smoked them, or steamed them in kelp wrappings in a pit lined with hot stones, as a welcome supplement to their eatables.

Again they were reduced to flinty pilot bread. Fresh

meat was once more an all-but-forgotten luxury. They shared their last dubious egg, making a sparse omelette of it, which they snapped up hungrily with their last two mouldy rashers of bacon.

On the evening of the day they ran out of sugar for their tea, Joe Busby's workboat poked its sleek nose around the lagoon's south point. Astern of it, riding jauntily in tow, was Lynn Hutchins' green carvel.

Joe killed his power. A stocky, bearded figure hobbled across the deck on crutches and, with Joe and Lynn helping, descended into the rowboat.

A querulous voice floated across the water. "Easy now! I ain't made of Injia-rubber!"

Lynn at the oars, the carvel headed for the beach. Ben Hutchins climbed out spryly enough, supporting himself on a crutch while his granddaughter held the boat steady with an oar dug into the shingle. Ben swung himself on his crutch through the shallows.

"He may need a hand over the driftlogs," Paddy said. "We'd better get down there."

But Ben emphatically did not welcome help. He freed a hand to warn them off with a vigorous flapping, which he backed with a glare.

"You two still here?" he grumbled at Paddy and Mayus. "Thought ye'd have had enough by now."

Ben studied them, frowning, while Lynn drew her boat farther up the beach. He wore a store-new blue work shirt and jeans with the creases still in them. On one foot was a new gumboot. The other, still enlarged by a dressing, was snugged into a heavy grey work sock.

"How's your foot, Ben?" Paddy asked.

He got a brusque answer. "Foot's fine. Would a' healed just as well without all that monkeydoodlin' in hospital."

Ben darted a sharp question. "I take it ye ain't catchin' fish?"

Paddy shook his head. "Guess we aren't cut out to be

handliners." He gave words to a painful decision that had been hardening in him as one luckless day followed another. "Mayus and me, we've been thinking. We're about ready to call it off."

Lynn Hutchins' reaction startled him. She stepped forward, a frown grooved deep between her eyes.

"Don't be in such a hurry," she said. "That's the trouble with boys, they've got no gumption. The fish are there. All you need is to know how to catch them!"

Ben nodded vigorously in agreement. "Ye've been doin' everything wrong." He advanced a lurching pace closer, dropping words emphatically. "Lord, boys, ye couldn't be makin' a worse hash of it if ye tried! Yer gear's all wrong. You chuff around towin' them goofy big spoons when you should be using herr'n-bait..."

"What's herr'n', Ben?" Paddy asked.

Lynn supplied a crisp answer. "Herring," she said. Then, waspishly, "Don't be so stupid."

"She's right," Ben told them. "That's what ye've been. Stupid! The plain fact is, I just don't see no hope for you without I take ye in hand."

"Will you do that, Ben?" Paddy asked eagerly. "Will you teach us how to handline?"

"We'd sure appreciate it, Ben," Mayus put in with unaccustomed humility.

The old man didn't answer. He turned and began to limp off toward his beehive shanty. Then he hesitated...halted, and swung awkwardly on his crutch to face Paddy and Mayus.

"I ain't goin' to guarantee it," said Ben in his cranky growl. "But if it can be done, we'll make handliners of ye."

"Call it payin' ye back for the help you gave me." Ben gave the bulky packsack on his shoulders a hitch. "I'll see you're rigged up properly. The girl there'll show you how to fish."

Ben limped on. Over his shoulder, he said, "Happens we got some steaks here. You boys want to come over an' help us eat them?"

Paddy gave Lynn a quick glance. Her Cheshire-cat smile had widened into a grin.

"Thanks, Ben," he said, and Mayus added a hearty, "That'd be great!"

Feeling lighter-hearted than he had for weeks, Paddy swung up a carton of the groceries they'd unloaded and trudged after Lynn and Ben toward the shanty.

Ben Hutchins proved to be a lavish host. He backed his thick steak with raw-fried potatoes, and opened a couple of cans of peas. Then he hauled an enormous cauliflower from a box, and two packaged apple pies.

After their lean weeks, Paddy found himself permanently hungry: he gorged to repletion, turning down Lynn's invitation to a third piece of pie only because he lacked the physical capacity.

Over Ben's growled protests, Paddy and Mayus helped Lynn with the washing up in a pan on the porch of the rickety abode. Presently Ben limped out to join them. He stood leaning on one crutch, the scarred brown fingers of his other hand hooked into his harness-strap belt.

"One o' yer troubles," Ben told them abruptly, "is you're too blamed late gettin' on the water. And you come in a sight too early. 'Cept for the change of tides, the two big bites of the day come at first light an' for a while after, then again in the evenin' just about the time you fellas have been comin' in. See you remember that."

"Yessir." Paddy stepped forward to steady Ben as he dropped his crutch and tried a cautious step.

"Stop it!" Ben ordered him in cantankerous tones. "Quit tryin' to baby me." Over his shoulder, he tossed another scrap of fishing know-how.

"You gotta study the tides an' the way salmon use 'em. Fer instance, there's no earthly use fishin' Diablo channel on the ebb. Only time she's hot is when a flood tide is bringing the bait in, and the bigger the flood the better. On the ebb, you want to fish the back eddies off the north an' south points, and out along Dragon Reef."

With a grunt of relief, Ben lowered himself into the tide-salvaged half barrel he had retooled and padded with gunny-sacking to make himself an armchair. He stretched his sore foot out and continued to hold forth.

"You gotta learn to fish at the right depth... Hell, there's so much you don't know, I doubt I could teach you in a month o' Sundays!"

"What about depth, Ben?" Paddy prompted; and Mayus came in like an echo. "Yeah, Ben, what are we doing wrong there?"

"Well, if you want to catch salmon, you need to think like a salmon. Now the coho, what the Yankees call a silver, he's your money-fish. He don't run very deep. You fish for him mostly in the top thirty foot of water, not way down near the bottom where you've been draggin' them heavy leads o' yours. Four ounces is plenty in these waters, except when they're feedin' just under the surface. Then you lighten up to two ounces or even less. Mebbee no lead at all."

Paddy listened intently. This was gospel propounded by a shellback rowboat fisherman. It could mean money in the bank.

"There's just one thing," Mayus put in. "We got no money. We can't buy the kind of riggin' Lynn uses. You know: the cane pole and big reel and all."

Ben Hutchins chuckled. He cocked an eye upward at the shanty rafters.

"Yeah?" he said. "Well, ain't that a pity!" Then, with a grin splitting his beard, "Look up there."

Paddy and Mayus peered upward. Across the rafters lay a wild tangle of equipment . . . oars, the long, thin slats of wood armed part way down one side with wire teeth which Paddy had heard called herring rakes, and half a dozen long cane poles with big wooden reels secured eighteen inches or thereabouts up their butts with a few turns of baling wire.

"Y' don't need any money, boys," Ben said. "S'pose ye just reach up there an' take yer pick?"

"But I don't get it," Paddy said. "Is all that stuff yours?"

"Is now," Ben told him. "At least the fellas that owned those outfits never come back to claim them." Ben settled his shoulders deeper into his barrel chair. Behind him, Lynn moved quietly abut her task of unpacking groceries and stowing them on crudely-fashioned shelves. "My, what a crew they was! Men, even a few women, headin' out in any rig that would float. I tell you. This used to be a right busy camp every summer. Most o' the shacks would have two, mebbe three handliners usin' it. They'd drift in from all up an' down the coast to fish the Diablos. By August there'd be easy forty of us, all waitin' for the big coho run."

"The big run?" Paddy asked.

"That's what I said," Ben told him. "You'd just about have given up hope of them coho comin' down the straits. Then you'd wake up one morning an' you'd hear the saucy rascals splashin' out there like crazy. The water'd be soupy with bait an' the air full of gulls an' cormorants and what-all, feastin' like there was no tomorrow."

"Is it ever still like that, Ben?" Mayus, sitting on the edge of a bunk with cheekbones leaned on fists, put the question dreamily.

Ben snorted. He shook his head in violent negative. "Naw! I'm talkin' about how it was back in the 'thirties. There ain't been a run like that fer a coon's age."

"Coon." Mayus smiled. "That's me! That's what my name means in white-man's talk."

"Well, coon or no," Ben said, "you ain't likely to see fishin' like that unless...unless..."

His voice trailed off. His eyes drooped. He was asleep.

Lynn stood behind her grandfather, hands on his shoulders. Her angular face was brooding.

"He's still weak," she said, "and he tires easily."

"Lynn?" Paddy put the question he'd been itching to ask. "Your grandfather. Why does he live away off here by his lone?"

"Simple." Lynn said. "He likes it here. Since my grandmother died, he can't stand to live in his big old house on Bukwis. Anyway, he was happy around here when he was a handliner."

Ben opened an eye. With an effort, he roused himself, to pick up his discourse where he'd broken it off.

"You won't see fishin' like that unless a real big northern run heads down coast. An' I'm not sitting up waitin' for that to happen!"

Paddy regarded Ben absently. The picture of those great past coho runs remained vivid behind his eyes.

"Anyway," he said, "Lynn still manages to make a stake handlining."

"Sure," Ben said. "By risin' early an' fishing late. An' by thinking like a fish, which you boys'll have to do."

Ben headed yawning from his armchair. "Now I'm gonna hit the hay. You two be on the beach with yer boats in the chuck before first light, understand? Lynn here will take ye out an' nursemaid ye."

Paddy broke the thoughtful silence as they walked back along the row of sagging, eyeless huts toward their own shack at the south end of the lagoon foreshore.

"Wonder how much Lynn does make?" he asked.

"Oh... Let's see..." Mayus did some figuring. S'pose

she's been averaging four salmon a day. At cannery prices, that'd fetch her around two-fifty, maybe three dollars.

Paddy too indulged in some mental arithmetic. His conclusion dismayed him. "At that rate," he said, "I haven't a chance of making enough to help my granddad. He's short eight hundred dollars."

"One thing you're forgetting," Mayus said.

"What's that?"

"The fall run. It could start any week now . . . any day." Mayus turned his head. His teeth flashed in a grin. "I know it's not too likely to be the way it was in the olden days. but there's always the chance we'll make it big!"

10

The Way to Make Them Come

In the pitch black of pre-dawn, Paddy and Mayus rolled groaning out of their bunks. They hustled into their clothes and, still yawning and rubbing the sleep from their eyes, stumbled down to launch their boats. Breakfast would have to wait: off in the east, Paddy saw, the sky was already shading from black to grey. Daybreak was near.

But early though they were, Lynn Hutchins was ahead of them, a shadow-shape silhouetted in her rowboat with the morning star a low-slung lamp above her.

"You're late," Lynn hailed them crossly. "I've been freezing here for half an hour!"

Lynn dipped her oars. Paddy and Mayus, in line astern, convoyed her toward the lagoon entrance. By the time they had stroked through the pass to the mirror-flat channel beyond, the morning star was paling and the sky was several shades lighter.

"What's the tide doing?" Lynn demanded.

"Jeez," Paddy said sheepishly, "I forgot to check."

"Well, it's ebbing," Lynn told him. "You should have known that. We'll pull over to Little Diablo reef and try the outer kelp. This tide, a pretty fair eddy makes up."

"What difference does an eddy make?" Paddy asked with careful humility. Lynn was a wasp of a girl, quick to sting.

"It packs the bait-fish in, and where there's bait is where you'll find salmon."

Afloat off the Little Diablo kelp, Paddy could see no sign of an eddy. He told Lynn so.

"You have to read the underwater as well as the surface," his teacher told him. She reached for her long and limber bamboo pole where it wagged over the carvel's stern. "This water's going around in a big circle." Paddy reached for his handline winder, but Lynn's sharp "No!" checked him.

"Forget about those silly lines," Lynn ordered him. "Watch while I bait up and maybe you'll learn something."

Yes, boss, Paddy murmured under breath. He laid his skiff gunwale to gunwale with Lynn's boat. On the other side, Mayus eased his dugout canoe alongside. They watched intently as Lynn reached a jam tin from under the stern thwart. In the tin, floating belly-up, were a dozen or so herring minnows.

"If you were to drink that," Lynn said with a jerk of her chin at the can, "or even take a sip of it, it'd lay you kicking." She reached into the tin and lifted out one of the limp minnows. "The thing is," she continued, "you can never count on raking live-bait to start your day's fishing. So you keep a few herring from the day before, in salt water with a dash of formaldehyde to preserve them." She gave Paddy a stern look. "You remember, though. Formaldehyde's deadly poison."

Paddy leaned from his skiff, craning to watch while

Lynn proceeded to free a small blue-steel hook from a reel stanchion. The hook was only half the size of the ones he and Mayus had been using. It was secured to a light silkworm gut leader about six feet long, which in turn was connected by a chain swivel to the heavier mainline packed on Lynn's large brassbound hardwood reel.

To Paddy, Lynn's cane pole with its wired-on guides and cumbersome reel seemed ponderous and old-fashioned. But he kept his mouth shut and followed every movement of Lynn's fingers as she threaded the herring minnow on her hook. Irrelevantly, it occurred to Paddy that Lynn had good hands—square in the palm, long-fingered and very brown.

"There's a trick to it," Lynn said. "You'll spoil a few herring before you get it." Her fingers gave the minnow a twist that brought it halfway around the hook-shank and seated it with tail projecting at a sharp angle.

"See how I put it on with a hump in its back and a kink in its tail? Lynn demanded. "That's so it will spin. You don't catch salmon unless your herring acts like a cripple."

Everything about Lynn's boat and gear, Paddy observed, was strictly functional. Behind her, leaned into a forked sapling thrust through a hole in the bow seat, her long, limber herring rake projected out past the carvel's nose. Also tucked behind within an over-the-shoulder reach was an enormous landing net.

The net frame had been cleverly shaped from a sapling with limbs growing out on either side. The limbs had been bent around and lashed together to form a wide-mouthed hoop. To this hoop was secured a deep and roomy bag of tarred brown herring netting.

A gaff, a heavy length of what looked to be yew-wood for a fish club, and a roll of gunnysacks thrust under the rowing thwart formed part of Lynn's equipment. There was also her bait can, a jug of drinking water wedged into the bows, and the inevitable plastic bailer. It was an outfit shaped to a purpose, without extras or frills. Paddy memorized each detail.

"Those sacks," Lynn said, following the direction of Paddy's glance. "You wet them down and cover your fish with them. Helps keep them in good condition. The cannery people are fussy. They won't buy old stale dried-out fish."

With a casual flip, Lynn tossed her herring-baited hook into the water. She swam it alongside for a minute, watching it intently to check its action. Then, satisfied, she let line peel off the reel drum. The herring dropped astern, a diminishing twinkle. When about fifteen feet of line had paid out, Lynn plunged a hand into her windbreaker pocket and brought out a small, keel-shaped sinker with a split ring at either end. She clipped the sinker to her line.

"With the light dim like it is," she said, "fish swim in the top water. That's where they'll find the bait. Later, when the sun brightens, I'll put on four ounces instead of the two I've got, and go deeper."

Between easy pulls on her oars, Lynn permitted more line to slip from her reel. Finally she gave the heavy brass wing-nut that regulated spool tension a twist that checked the outflowing line.

"You have to keep changing your depth and speed," she told Paddy and Mayus, who shadowed along on either side of her boat. "Right now, I've got exactly forty feet of line out. I can tell that by the markers I wrapped on my line. Later, if fish don't come, I'll try it longer or shorter."

She settled to her oars, easing her smooth-planked hull through the water with minimum effort and scarce a ripple.

"The thing is," she concluded her dissertation, "you've got to put that herring where the salmon are. If you don't, you might as well be fishing in a bathtub."

They cruised on along the island shoreline, a hundred feet or so out from the reef-studded jungle of kelp whose slick brown bulbs and trailing fronds threw random gleams in the strengthening light.

With no warning other than a creak of strained fibers, Lynn's cane pole whipped over into a hoop. Out astern of her boat, something splashed and flurried, tossing spray.

Lynn scooped up her pole with one swift reach. Holding the tip high, she seized the line between reel and first guide, and began to strip it into the boat bottom in a series of powerful yanks. Silver flashed and skittered toward the boat.

A last lunge fetched the fish alongside, its head held clear of the water by the pressure of Lynn's arched pole, its tail lashing futilely. Lynn darted a hand over her shoulder for her landing net. Holding the strain on the pole with one fist, she shook out the mesh, then reached it overside in an easy, scooping dip. She lifted the net with silver sagging and glittering in the meshes—a fat coho salmon about twenty-six inches long, whose weight Paddy's envious eyes guessed at six pounds.

Lynn whacked her fish across its sharp predator's snout with her club, twisted the hook loose from its jaw-corner, and slithered the coho on to the bottomboards. Then she reached for her minnow can, rebaited with a flick of her fingers, and in a matter of seconds was back in business with another bait paying astern.

It had been a smooth, deadly-efficient process, conducted with machine-like speed.

"Boy," Paddy said, "you didn't waste any time playing that one, did you?"

Lynn frowned across at him. "You talk like a sport," she said. "This isn't fun, it's business. When fish are coming, you've got to be fast if you want to make a killing."

Again, she cinched the wing-nut on her reel. "Did you watch how I brought it in? Locked my reel spool and skidded it in so fast it never had a chance to cut up rough."

Paddy made a mental note to do likewise. This wasn't the sportsman's way: but Lynn was right. They were not fishing for sport. He was learning by the minute.

Lynn boated three more coho, all of a size with her first, before the sun had cleared the distant mainland snowpeaks. With the sun balanced, a fiery ball, in the notch of a mountain, the bite ceased as abruptly as it had begun.

Lynn wound in her line. "I'm getting hungry," she announced. "Do you guys have any food?"

Paddy shook his head. "A bit of pilot bread. Some tea."

"Then you'd better eat with us," Lynn invited.

Mayus protested half-heartedly. "Jeez, Lynn, we can't do that. You had us to dinner..."

But Lynn cut him off with an impatient flip of her hand.

"In a fish camp," she said, "It's share and share alike. My granddad taught me that as well as how to fish." She reached for her oars, and with Paddy and Mayus tagging after, set a course for the home lagoon.

They were skirting Diablo's south reef when Lynn paused in her rowing. She peered intently overside. Then with a smooth backward reach, she lifted her twelve-foot herring rake from its sapling fork and dipped its needle-armed end into the satin-smooth water. She swung the rake in a fore-and-aft stroke that sank in deep. As she lifted it from the water, Paddy saw that for a yard or more from its end, one side of the rake gleamed with

wriggling silver. On each of the sharp piano-wire needles let into the wood like teeth, a herring minnow glittered.

Lynn freed the minnows with a vigorous shake of her rake to skip and bounce on the tarpaulin spread forward of the rowing thwart. Then she dipped again, made another canoe-paddler's stroke, and brought up another squirming freight of live bait.

Looking over the side of his skiff, eyes squinted against the sun-dazzle, Paddy saw that the water twinkled with living silver. Those random flashes, close-packed, indicated a herring school swimming industriously along in the shadow of the kelp.

Lynn got in three more swift and graceful passes, each of which brought up a trove of minnows. On the fourth pass, the rake came up with a lone herring impaled. The school had sounded. Lynn gathered the minnows into her jam tin. She renewed the water with a dip overside, then plunged a hand into her windbreaker and tugged out a small bottle. Prominent on its label was a black skull and crossbones.

Lynn unscrewed the bottle cap with finicky care, then shook a few sparing drops of formaldehyde into her bait can. She replaced the bottle top, pocketed the bottle, and shoved the doctored tin of minnows under the stern-sheets where they'd be shaded from the sun's heat.

"That'll give me a start for this evening," she said. Yawning, she reached for her oars.

After breakfast, Lynn retired to her bunk in the cedar-shake annex tacked on to the shanty. Ben Hutchins lifted a shotgun—a large, old-fashioned pump action repeater—from pegs behind the door.

"Gonna see if I can collect a bird or two," he said to the boys as he stepped past them. "You help yourselves to any o' that fishin' gear up there."

"Birds?" Paddy looked up enquiringly from his second cup of coffee.

"Yeah. Willow grouse. This island's buzzin' with 'em . . . guess they got blown over from Bukwis. Or flew over, maybe."

Ben sauntered off, shotgun cradled under one arm, leaving Paddy and Mayus to haul handliners' tackle down from the rafters.

They picked and chose among the long cane poles, selecting two that were less warped than the others. The wire that secured the brass-and-walnut reels to the rod butts had long ago rusted almost to powder; the reels broke away from the cane as the boys struggled to crank spools frozen fast by years of disuse.

"We got any oil?" Paddy asked as he strained on a reel-handle.

"Nope." Mayus thought for a moment, forehead puckered, then came up with a solution. "I'll bet bear grease would work, though."

They rooted out a can of bear-fat drippings from under the washup bench on their porch, pried the reels apart with the help of the screwdriver blade on Paddy's scout knife, and gave the innards a liberal cleaning and greasing. Paddy turned a reel handle. The spool revolved, stiffly at first, then more easily, until he could spin it with a flick of his finger. Good enough! But the line with which the reel was packed proved to be stiff as wire — a frayed, opaque and entirely unmanageable strand such as Paddy had never seen before.

"Wonder what this stuff is?" he asked Mayus, tugging a foot of the springy line off the reel.

Ben Hutchins' voice startled him. Ben stood in the doorway, a brace of willow grouse dangling by their necks from one hand, his shotgun laid across his other arm.

"That there's called Japanese gut," he said. "It's mis'able

stuff, but until they invent something better, it's all we got."

Ben racked his gun on pegs behind the door, hung his birds on another peg, and seated himself on the edge of a bunk. He groped in the chest pocket of his faded shirt and brought out a short-stemmed, blackened pipe. But he didn't light the pipe: just sat at ease, watching Paddy and Mayus while they worked.

"Stick your reels in a bucket of water overnight," Ben advised. "That way, the Japanese gut'll soften enough to fish with." The pipe tilted till the bowl all but touched his nose. He added, "Happens I got a few silkworm gut leaders in my gear. You c'n help yourselves."

"Thanks, Ben," Paddy said with a quick smile. And Mayus, "We'll pay you back when we hit fish."

"Don't thank him," Lynn put in tartly from where she sat stitching a pair of already much-mended jeans. "Those are my leaders. See you pay me back."

"Real snappin'-turtle, ain't she?" Ben murmured. He watched while Paddy lashed his reel back on the rod butt with a length of codline.

"That outfit you got there," Ben said to Paddy. "It b'longed to a big redhead we called 'Saskatchewan', him bein' a prairie gopher from Regina. He joined the Merchant Marine when war come, an' got torpedoed off Ireland." Ben sighed for days gone over. "Lord," he said, "I can see him now, skiddin' the coho in with that old Calcutta cane! I expect ye'll find his initials burned into the butt."

"Who owned mine?" Mayus asked, his fingers busy with codline.

"Let's see..." Ben craned from his bunk to squint. "I think that was One-Eye Pete's riggin'. Yeah, it was his, all right. There's his brand, see? The circle-an'-cross. He was real catty, that fella. One day off the Little Diablo kelp, 'bout this time of year, Pete hit the big run comin' down from the north. Right in the slot, he was." Ben's voice was abstracted, his gaze absent, as he relived those bumper years. "One-Eye Pete, he caught a hundred-twenty-six coho between first light an' moonrise. Caught 'em on the big brass spinner he favoured. Had to bring his boat in twice, practic'lly swamped with the load in it, an' dump his salmon."

Paddy and Mayus listened, hands arrested. The thought of catching that many fish in a day was fantastic.

"Guess they paid him pretty good," Mayus ventured.

"Not so's you'd notice," Ben said, his thoughts still deep in the past. "Coho in them years brought us three-four cents a pound, dressed. Say about two-bits a fish. Took a lot o' coho to make a man a stake."

"He must have been real good," Paddy said a little wistfully. "It must have been great, being a handliner then!" In his mind's eye he could see the camp with its shacks in repair . . . with a fleet of rowboats on the lagoon beach, and fishermen like Saskatchewan and One-Eye Pete coming and going. A little town: a busy place.

"Yeah, it was good," Ben said. "It was just about the best time I've ever known." Ben groped a kitchen match from his shirt, popped it on his thumbnail and applied the flame to his pipe-bowl. His voice came through to them in a cloud of acrid smoke.

"Y'know," he said solemnly, "I guess I'm just about the last o' the oldtime handliners, an' I hardly fish anymore. Can't stand the gaff."

Mayus still brooded on the glory days. "That man who caught all the salmon," he asked. "One-Eye Pete. How'd he get all those fish to the cannery?"

Ben chuckled. "He didn't. In them years, the cannery came to us. All through the season, May to the end of September, they'd keep a buyer's scow anchored in the cove. Had a little store on board where you could buy fishin' gear an' tobacco an' grub, or a cane pole for a quarter. Anything a boy needed."

Paddy got to his feet, his cane pole rigged and ready.

"All set," he declared. "You think it's any use us heading out now, Ben?"

"Too early," Ben said. "Besides, you still ain't got landin' nets."

"Thought we'd borrow a couple of those up there," Paddy told him, with a nod at the laden rafters.

"Too old an' brittle," Ben said. "You don't want your net handle bustin' off with a fish in the mesh, do you? Y' better go up in the woods an' cut new frames. . . . I got plenty of herr'n twine for the bags."

It cost Paddy and Mayus an hour of hard searching until, in an evergreen thicket back of the spring, they found a couple of saplings which would fill the bill. Obviously, nature considered slender trunks with limbs growing out exactly opposite each other as the rarest of flukes. They had to settle for less-than-perfect frames. Trimming the handles to size, bending the net arms around and lashing them into wide-mouthed hoops, occupied most of their afternoon. By the time they'd tied on the mesh bags Ben provided, evening was upon them.

"You c'n eat when you pull in," Ben decreed. "Right now, she's fishin' time."

Separated by half a sea-mile, the boats loafed across calm water. Paddy's cane pole wagged over the stern of his skiff, its butt tucked under his thigh. His net was a quick snatch away; his herring rake, down from the rafters with the cobwebs dusted off it, slanted like a bowsprit past the skiff's nose.

Lynn had shared her herring minnows with them. Paddy spoiled several of the bright little fish in his attempts to bait up with the turn-and-twist that would guarantee a seductively-spinning lure. Finally he succeeded after a fashion. At least, when towed alongside, his herring twirled and twinkled.

He clipped a four-ounce sinker, a loan from Lynn's stock, to his line, and let gut slip off his reel until an estimated thirty feet towed astern. Then he resumed his oars. His pole-tip nodded gently to the pull and throb of the bait. A tingle of excitement fingered his spine. He was handlining the right way, this time—the way that should put salmon in his boat!

The evening deepened. His bait spun through the depths unmolested. Paddy rowed on, excitement gradually giving way to disappointment. He'd firmly expected to be tied to a coho long ago.

Lynn Hutchins put her green carvel into a parallel course.

"Got any?" Paddy hollered across to her.

For answer, Lynn flipped up three fingers. "How about you?"

"Nothing," Paddy told her glumly.

"How much line have you out?"

"Thirty feet," Paddy called back. "Just like you had this morning."

"Well, it isn't morning now," Lynn told him crisply. "Hasn't my granddad told you that you've got to think like a fish? When the water's this flat, coho can get spooky. You're fishing too close to your boat. Let out another twenty or thirty feet."

Paddy inspected his bait, then, trying hard to think like a fish, he paid out line until a generous sixty feet trailed astern. He resumed his oars, not really expecting a change in his luck. He was doomed to fish on forever, a galley slave chained to his oars, and catch nothing...

His pole whipped down. The butt bore hard against

his leg. Out behind the skiff, a shining fish-shape took to the air in a flurrying leap.

"Fish on!!!" Paddy vented his delight in a full-lunged howl. He snatched up his rod, elevating it as he had seen Lynn do, until his fish bucked and strained against the bowed and creaking cane.

He reached for his line, meaning to strip his coho in as he had seen Lynn do that morning. But the fish was now heading jet-propelled seaward. The line burned through his fingers, came up hard against the locked reel spool. Only the length and yielding whippiness of the cane kept the leader from popping.

Thoroughly demoralized, Paddy wrestled with pole and reel. He was dimly aware that Lynn had eased closer, and that Mayus, on his other side in his slim canoe, was rocking and hugging himself with glee.

"Ride 'im cowboy!" Mayus yelled, and went off into a cackle of laughter.

Somehow — he never quite knew how — Paddy worked his fish alongside. He made a clumsy lunge with his net, holding the cane reared back in his other hand . . . missed, dipped again, and felt the live and solid weight of his coho in the meshes.

Paddy swung the net inboard. He clubbed his fish, knowing a pang for the taking of a life so vibrant, then held it up for inspection.

"It'll go eight pounds," Lynn told him. "Maybe nine."

Mayus's voice came across the water-gap. "I'm one up on you, boy! I got two!"

With shaking fingers, Paddy rebaited. He got his rig out again and fishing. Before he had rowed fifty yards, he was into another coho. With his lesson learned, he skidded this one to the boat before it could commence to fight, and got his net under it neatly enough.

Fishing on in the twilight, his skiff whispering over

sunset-painted water with the islands in dark silhouette and the mainland hills deep purple in the distance, Paddy dipped his oars with a full heart.

He'd made it. He had taken two fine coho, with handliner's gear in the handliners' old way. Now, he told himself, he was home free. Now, nothing could stop him! Paddy drew a deep breath of evening air cooling for night. Yes, and it was good to have Mayus and Lynn, his friends, sharing his luck . . .

The thought checked him. Lynn, his friend? He pondered on that, groping toward a conclusion that surprised him. Somehow or other, since they'd taken Ben with his hurt foot over to the cannery in the teeth of a blow, Lynn's status had changed. In her own prickly, chip-on-shoulder way, she had become a friend . . . and Paddy found himself glad of that.

11

Where Have All the Salmon Gone?

Paddy was bone-weary when he pulled in to the home lagoon in the late dusk. Four coho salmon, like in size as peas in a pod, gleamed silver on the bottomboards of his skiff.

Mayus and Lynn rowed in behind him. Mayus had five fish in his black canoe: there was no telling how many Lynn had taken.

"Boy, am I pooped out!" Mayus called, echoing Paddy's feelings. "Why don't we leave these fish till morning? Then clean them and run 'em over to the cannery."

Lynn's voice, coming crisply from the shadows, nipped that lazy-man's notion.

"If you want top dollar, those fish had better be gutted and delivered tonight." She added with a certain smugness, "That's what I mean to do with my seven."

Lynn eased her rowboat's nose on to the shingle. She heaved her catch overside, then clambered out of the boat to crouch with knife in fist.

Sighing, Paddy and Mayus followed Lynn's example.

Handlining, Paddy brooded as he knelt with knife in hand and fish blood smeared to his elbows, was a lot more than lazing along in a skiff on a warm summer day. It also entailed long days and hard work, to be plugged away at when all you wanted was to grab a meal and roll into your blankets.

Fish dressed and bundled in wet gunnysacks, they rowed in convoy across the channel to Bukwis Island cannery. The fish-processing plant blazed with lights. As they pulled into the cove, they could hear the steady purr-and-thud of its battery of machines. Half a dozen seiners and gillnetters were tied on at the floats, along with a couple of tall-poled trollers. Paddy looked for his friend Gus Sorensen's *Westerly* in the crowded rank, but failed to spot her. Gus, he supposed, was off fishing the northern grounds.

Big Joe Busby strolled down from his office to greet them. "We're busy as all get-out," Joe told them. "Got a big run of pinks dumped on us." He peered into Lynn's carvel where it lay snugged to a float. "I suppose you expect me to buy those sprats of those?"

"Better fish than your pinks," Lynn answered, "What kind of thieve's price are you paying today?"

"Fish look sort of stale to me," Joe retorted, bent and squinting critically. "You had 'em laying around long?"

"Mister Busby," Lynn said with stiff dignity, "if those cohos were any fresher, they'd be flapping their tails. And you darn well know it!"

Joe gave Paddy and Mayus a wink. Obviously, this sparring was a game that he and Lynn enjoyed. Joe said to Paddy, "I see you boys have been hitting 'em too. Well, you got a good teacher." He grinned at them. "Crabby, but knows her stuff!"

Later, Paddy and Mayus sauntered along the dock from

the cannery office, each with a small but comfortable wad of bills tucked away in his jeans. Joe had asked them if they'd take cheques. Then, noting their long faces, he had opened his safe and brought out cash money.

Paddy and Mayus parted company with Joe at the head of the dock. In the store, they cut their bill by almost half. With the rest of their cash, they bought gear to replace their borrowings from Lynn, and the food supplies they so badly needed.

"Broke again," Mayus said cheerfully as they headed back toward the float-string. "Feels natural."

A new work craft, Paddy observed, had added itself to the fleet at the float-string. His heart gave a bump. It was the ill-kept black drum-seiner that they'd helped thwart in the creek-robbing raid on Cormorant Cove.

Paddy saw that Red Dunc Sloan and Arnie Peters had replaced the burned net with another. They lounged on deck, Red Dunc with a shoulder propped against the wheelhouse.

They didn't speak, but their eyes followed Paddy and Mayus as they passed. It was not a friendly survey. Deliberately, Arnie Peters spat overside.

"Those two give me the shivers," Mayus muttered. "It's like passing a cage of tigers." He glanced at the black seiner and asked uneasily, "You think they know we turned 'em in?"

"Who cares!" Paddy replied, with a hardihood he didn't really feel.

"I do," Mayus said. "I sure don't want those two on my tail."

But already, Paddy's thought's were elsewhere. He found himself, to his immense surprise, disappointed that Lynn hadn't stuck around. It occurred to him with a distinct shock that they were no longer two but three, and that he kind of missed that razor-tongued coppertop.

A discordant jangling erupted around him. Paddy checked in mid-stride and snatched the rucksack off his back.
The jangling continued. While Mayus gaped at him,
Paddy unbuckled the rucksack flap. He reached into the
bag and pulled out a large, nickle-plated alarm clock
which continued to blast away until his fingers found the
shut-off knob.

"What's that for?" Mayus asked.

"To get us up in the morning," Paddy said. "Before
daylight." He added grimly as he stuffed the alarm clock
in his rucksack, "If that won't, nothing will!"

The alarm clock's hellish din jolted them out of their
bunks and into the next day's pre-dawn gloom. They
snatched a ration of pilot bread and jam, washed it down
with gulps of cold coffee, then stumbled to their boats.
Early though they were, Lynn was still out ahead of
them. They could hear the gentle splash of her oars and
see her rowboat, a gliding shadow that receded across the
star-mirroring lagoon.

The rowing thwart seemed twice as hard at this un-
chancy hour of the day. It was also wet with dew. Paddy's
hands were stiff from yesterday's long spell at the oars.
Not until he was clear of the lagoon entrance and cruis-
ing north along Diablo channel did his fingers limber up.

Lynn, he remembered, had told them that the channel
was a hot-spot on a flooding tide—and tide was now
making toward the full.

With a tingle of anticipation, Paddy reached under the
stern thwart for his bait can. A lone herring minnow
floated belly-up in the formaldehyde mix. Well, no matter! He'd soon rake more.

Paddy baited up with the handliner's twist which now
came more naturally to his fingers, and flipped his rig
overside. He settled to the oars, feeling the strong tide

that flooded south down the channel working busily against him.

The skiff eased past one of the innumerable rocky headlands with a pattering of ripples under its nose. Paddy, gaze glued to his pole, saw its tip give a sharp and sudden lurch. But nothing hooked itself—there was no leap-and-splash astern—and after a tense moment he reached for his outfit and winched in his line.

The herring minnow was still on his hook, but its shape had changed. It had been pulled so that it lay straight along the hook-shank. Also, its after portion from back fin to tail had been neatly peeled of skin. Something had mouthed his bait...but what?

He shrugged the problem away, and was reaching for his bait tin when he remembered: no more herring!

Nothing for it but to rake up a fresh supply. Paddy eased along, oars dipping gently, while he scouted over the side. But the breeze-ruffle which had come up with the sun thwarted his vision. There could be a skillion herring swimming down under, and he wouldn't be able to spot them.

Two hours later, hot, frustrated and thoroughly out of sorts, Paddy was still searching for bait. The sight of Lynn Hutchins across the water, sitting in her carvel with cane pole bowed while she yarded a coho to her net, failed to improve Paddy's outlook.

But since misery loves company, he did feel a gloomy satisfaction when Mayus's dugout ghosted alongside.

Mayus's bottomboards were innocent of fish. His bait can was also empty.

"No herring," he said needlessly, "and I can't locate 'em."

Mayus jerked his chin in Lynn's direction. "She found them. She was raking 'em in like sixty, the darn otter!"

"Okay," Paddy said. "But I'm not going to ask her. She's babied us too much already."

"Then what are we gonna do?" Mayus demanded. "We can't catch fish without bait."

"We'll just have to keep looking," Paddy snapped back at him.

Poking along the fringe of a kelp bed, Paddy finally caught a broken shimmer of silver deep beneath the surface. But by the time he had scrambled his oars inboard, freed his herring rake and clattered it overside, the school was long departed.

Paddy worked his skiff deeper into the kelp forest. In a nook among glistening kelp bulbs, he spotted more silver twinkling. He dipped the rake, trying to achieve Lynn's easy grace. But it was a swashing, splashy reach, and his rake came up empty.

Paddy shot a glance at Mayus. On the other side of the little bay, Mayus knelt in the bows of his canoe, butt in air and rake balanced crossways in both hands. Using the rake as a paddle, Mayus dipped in alternate strokes on either side. Then all of a sudden he made a long reach forward, drove his rake deep, and stroked it aft along the canoe side. When the rake had lifted from the water behind Mayus, half a dozen lively herring minnows glittered on its teeth.

Mayus loosed a jubilant war-whoop. He shook the minnows off his rake and scrabbled them into his bait tin.

"We're in business!" he shouted across the water to Paddy. "Want some?"

With a sudden warmth, Paddy knew that the offer was instinctive — part of the Kwakiutl philosophy that refused to hoard and that took open-handed generosity for granted in a friend.

"Thanks," Paddy called back. "But I'd better learn how myself!"

"Then try it my way," Mayus called back. "It works."

Paddy moved up into the nose of his skiff. There he

knelt in precarious balance, peering down with the rake balanced across his palms. Almost at once, his eyes caught the shimmering undulations of schooled herring. He was about to lower the rake when, on the edges of the school and below it, he saw other, very much larger fish-shapes. He realized those long, lazily gliding shadows were coho salmon. They were herding the herring school along like so many border collies shepherding a batch of woollies.

Absorbed, paddling gently with his rake to keep pace with the school, Paddy continued to peer down. As he watched, a herring minnow detached itself from the school and darted off at a tangent. Instantly, one of the coho lunged off-station. Paddy saw the fish's jaws close on the minnow. But only for an instant. The jaws parted and the herring was expelled, to wabble off into the depths. Before it vanished, Paddy saw that its rear section had been neatly peeled of skin.

So that was what had happened to his bait! Paddy added the scrap of knowledge to his handliner's bag of tricks, with a mental note to ask Lynn or her grandfather how one coaxed a coho so finicky into striking. Then he settled to the serious business of renewing his bait supply.

When another herring school shimmered across his bows, he was ready. He dipped deep, passed the rake astern, and fetched it up — this time with a dozen minnows trapped on the teeth. After that, the bait-raking went very well. A few more passes and his can held several dozen weakly-finning minnows.

The early-morning bite was over — he had lost that — but the tide was close to changing, and Lynn had instructed them to work the change of tides. Paddy buckled down to the oars, shooting the skiff cross-channel on a course for the south point of Little Diablo and the eddy in which bait-fish were crowded together by the circling waters.

He had no sooner rounded the point than he was into a fish. He lost that one, managing to knock it off the hook as he reached to net it. But another coho struck hard while he was letting out a fresh bait.

For about twenty minutes the biting remained brisk. When a lull did develop, Paddy saw with pleased surprise that five coho were adding their sequin-bright shed scales to the spangling on his bottomboards.

He fished a while longer. Then, prodded by hunger, he set a course back for camp. But, with a lesson learned, he gutted his catch and stowed it in the shade under wet sacking before he tended to his own wants.

Paddy was hacking thick slices off a loaf while canned meatballs and spaghetti bubbled in a saucepan when Mayus stepped into the shack. Mayus's face wore an overall grin.

"How'd you make out?" Mayus asked. Then, not waiting for an answer, "I got four!"

"One up on you," Paddy said, returning Mayus's smile. At this rate, they'd have cleaned up their store debt and be making real money in no time!

After lunch, Paddy tramped down the foreshore and over the rock point to Ben's and Lynn's shack. Lynn, he saw, had prettied its single window up with a brightly-patterned curtain.

Nobody home. He was turning away when footsteps crunched on gravel, and he turned to find Ben and Lynn coming up from the beach. Ben carried a long-handled spade over one shoulder.

"After clams?" Paddy asked.

Lynn beat her grandfather to an answer. "We were looking for camas lily bulbs. They eat almost as good as potatoes."

"Find any?" Paddy asked.

"No," Lynn said. Then, in a quick change of subject, "Did you want something?"

Paddy told about his experience with the herring-skinning coho. Ben listened, leaning on his spade; Lynn trudged on toward the shanty.

"What you could do," Ben said, "is dangle an extra hook a couple of inches below the baited one. Sometimes that'll put the rascals on. Or you could try a water-breaker."

Paddy fired the inevitable question. "What's a water-breaker?"

For answer, Ben thrust a hand in a pocket. He pulled out a handful of change in which was mixed an assortment of red rubber discs, each with a hole punched through its centre.

"These here are water-breakers," he said. "You slip one on the leader above the hook. It gingers up yer minnow's action . . . gives her a reg'lar dipsy-doodle. "He added sternly, "I ain't gonna give you these. But I'll fix you up with a chunk of inner tube so's you can cut yer own. An' you'd best have some formaldehyde too, only don't waste it! You won't find any more this side of the nearest drug-store, an' that's fifty miles away."

Rooting about in the trash heap back of their own shack, Paddy and Mayus turned up a couple of empty pill bottles. Into each, Lynn decanted a sparing supply of her precious formaldehyde. She also insisted that, with a stub of black pencil from her grandfather's packrat trove, the boys inscribe large skulls and crossbones on each bottle label.

"If you were to treat yourselves to a nip of that rat tonic by mistake," she explained, "It would be the end of you!"

Ben got up from where he sprawled, pipe between teeth, on his bunk.

"Better hustle yer fish over to the cannery," he advised, "whilst you're able."

Startled, Paddy looked up from inscribing eye-sockets on his glaring skull.

"Why, Ben?" he asked. "Why not tonight after the fishing?"

You won't be fishin' tonight," Ben told him. "The weather's fixin' to haul down. When coho start fussin' with the bait an' when the gulls dip their faces in the saltchuck, it's a certain-sure sign."

Ben pocketed his pipe. "You too, granddaughter," he said to Lynn. "You'll just have time to get over an' back before she's whoopin' round yer ears."

When they shot the lagoon pass on the return trip, their morning catch delivered and paid for, it was in flight from a prickling sea the colour of gunmetal, flecked by the first hostile whitecaps.

Ben's weather prediction was dead-on. By dark, a forty-knot blow was howling and whining around the shacks.

Paddy and Mayus huddled close to an oil-drum stove stoked with beach-gathered slabs of Douglas fir bark until its sides glowed cherry-red. They consoled themselves for the loss of the evening fishing with mugs of cocoa and hunks of buttery bread slathered with strawberry jam. That jam and the cocoa were luxuries: their morning's catch had cleared their debt at the store. Now, when they got back to their fishing, they'd be free and clear to work on their stake,

Lying in his bunk, warm in his blankets, Paddy listened to the drumming of rain on the cedar shakes overhead. He let his mind go roving.

He thought of his grandfather with affection and a twinge of worry. The tough old Scotsman worked cruelly hard. He even spared a thought or two for home, which seemed incredibly distant and part of some other, easier and more ordered life. He hoped young Sheba, his Airedale pup, was working out all right. By the time he got back to resume school in the fall, Sheba ought to be past the slipper-mauling stage and ready for training. His last conscious thought was of his mother.

Take care, she'd urged him in her last letter. *Eat properly. If you get your feet wet, be sure you change your shoes . . .*

Paddy smiled to himself in the dark. It was just as well, he reflected drowsily, that mothers didn't know everything!

The gale lingered on as a three-day southeaster. It banged, it ranted, it blew smoke down their stovepipe chimney and it kept the passage in a white lather. Then it subsided as quickly as it had roared in.

But when they ventured to launch their boats in the fourth dawn, and to fish their way across a mountainous but smooth-topped swell which was the gale's aftermath, it was to find their fishing grounds empty of coho. The little run had moved on, leaving a vacuum behind it.

And as one luckless day followed another, this melancholy condition showed no sign of changing. Paddy even found himself wondering a time or two whether the brisk fishing they'd enjoyed previously had been merely a random fluke of nature, unlikely to be repeated.

"We're not doing so good," Paddy said soberly. He had rowed in from yet another long and fishless day. Mayus tagged astern to beach his canoe beside Paddy's skiff.

"Sure aren't," Mayus agreed. "You know, I've been thinking. Wondering if we shouldn't maybe try another area. Get one of the trollers, maybe Gus if he's in, to give us a tow north."

"It's an idea," Paddy said. He pondered for a moment:

maybe in a new location, their luck would change for the better. "Tell you what," he said. "Let's ask Ben what he thinks."

What Ben thought threatened to scorch the air around them.

"You're no better'n a couple o' hoppergrasses," Ben accused them, head thrust out to emphasize his words. "Skippin' here, hoppin' there . . . Why, this is just about the best handlining ground on the coast! What you gotta do is stick to it. Stay out there. Keep yer lines in the water. Sooner or later, I expect them coho will show up."

Ben reflected for a moment, leaning on the spade that seemed to accompany him on all his wanderings. Then he said, with obvious reluctance, "Unless this happens to be one o' them freak years when the run don't show at all. Happens that way once in a while, 'specially now that fish is a lot scarcer than they used to be."

"Does it happen often?" Paddy shot the question anxiously.

"Nope," Ben said. "Matter o' fact, I c'n just remember two times the fish didn't come. It meant hungry days for a handliner, I tell ye! No stake to last me through the winter. Ben's frown deepened. "It was awful!" he said in shocked tones. "Why, I like to have starved if Joe Busby hadn't found me a job ashore. B'lieve me, I enjoyed about as much misery as I could stand."

Paddy and Mayus trudged up to their shack in thoughtful mood. Finally Paddy broke the silence.

"We'll give it another week," he said. "If that's all right with you."

"Okay," Mayus agreed. "One more week. Then we shove off."

"We'll try somewhere else," Paddy said, with more optimism than he felt. "Maybe hit it good."

"Not me," Mayus said. He halted to face Paddy with a scowl between his eyes, and his mouth corners pulled down. "If they don't show in a week, I'm quitting."

12

To Feed a Boy in China

Their fishless days continued. Once more, the food level in their grub box subsided until they were scraping bottom, with scant hope of replenishment unless they chose to renew their debt to Mrs. Busby at the cannery store. Nor could they look to Lynn or Ben for help, even if their pride permitted. Those two were no better off than they.

They settled into a deadly routine. Up before dawn, out through the pass to the wide waters beyond, row all day with only a break for the nosebag lunches they brought with them. Those lunches oftener than not consisted of a cold rock cod fillet left over from last night's sparse supper. With hopes at rock bottom, they fished their drearily familiar courses until dusk moved in, then pulled wearily for home.

They were rawhide-tough now, so lean that each rib showed, and so deeply tanned that even the fiercest refraction of light rays from sun on salt water couldn't burn them. Their shirts, when they bothered to wear shirts, were ragged, their jeans crudely patched and salt-bleached.

Without realizing it, Paddy had turned into a skilled smallboat man. Now the occasional day of wind and running sea no longer kept them ashore. They fished through weather they wouldn't have dared venture out in at the start, and they learned the sheltered nooks in the kelp jungles where they could count on finding bait even when the sea ran choppy.

On the fifth day, they landed in glum silence. Paddy squatted by the water's edge to fillet the rock cod dredged up from a kelp reef that would give them their dinner.

Ben Hutchins came to stand over him. The continued absence of salmon had reduced even Ben's stubborn optimism.

"Don't know when I last seen a season so mis'able," he said. He cleared his throat noisily. "Looks like that leetle boy down in China is gonna go hungry."

Paddy tossed the stripped-down rock cod carcass to his coterie of hungrily-kibitzing seagulls. "What boy?" he asked. "What are you nattering about?"

"Y' don't have to be snappish," Ben told him. "T'ain't my fault the fish don't come."

"Sorry," Paddy said. Then, prompting, "What about that boy in China?"

Ben lowered himself onto his heels. "Well," he said, "it's kind of a dream I had. It's as if I was lookin' down between my feet clean through the earth to the other side, see? An' there's this leetle upside-down Chinese boy with chopsticks in one hand an' a can of prime British Columbia red coho salmon in the other. That boy is havin' himself a feast." Ben paused. He rasped in his throat again, then said impressively, "Y'know who caught that salmon? You did. Or maybe young Mayus. Or maybe my girl, Lynn. Handlined it right out of Diablo Channel to feed a kid on the other side of the world. Made me feel real good, I tell ye!"

Ben's brown hand went out to cuff Paddy's ankle. It was a gesture that offered rough comfort.

"What I'm gettin' at, boy, is you gotta keep fishin'. If you don't come up with salmon, people could go hungry."

It was a primitive, even a childish philosophy. But somehow Paddy found it reassuring.

"Thanks, Ben," he said. He rocked off stiff knees, cod fillets dangling from one hand. "But don't worry. I'm not giving up."

"Hell, it's not you I'm worryin' about," Ben said. "But I figure your sidekick has just about had it."

Late that night, Paddy found himself awake in his bunk and listening. He couldn't be sure what had roused him: he only knew there had been something—some minor change in the tenor of the night.

He rolled out of his blankets and went to stand in the shack doorway. Dawn wasn't too far off, even though the morning star still hung like a lamp over the quiet sea.

The sound came from the sea. It was as if the water itself gave off a very low rustle that kept on and on.

Puzzled, Paddy listened until the late-night chill set him shivering. Then, with the mystery unsolved, he returned to the warmth of his blankets.

The alarm clock roused him with its clattering toxin.

Groaning, he swung his legs out, giving a poke to the underside of the top bunk as he did so.

Usually Mayus, who slept like a cat, was up before the alarm. But not this day, even though he was awake.

Mayus said, "I'm not going out."

"How come?" Paddy asked. Then in quick worry, "You're not sick, are you?"

"I'm okay," Mayus said. "I've just had it, that's all."

"Aw. Come on . . ." Paddy began: but Mayus cut him short.

"It's no use," he said. "Handlining's for the birds. I'm sick to the teeth with never catching anything." Mayus rolled over and tugged his blankets around his ears. "I'm through." His voice came muffled from under the covers. "I knew there'd be no luck on a dead people's island. I'm heading back to Bukwis this morning."

With a heavy heart, Paddy tramped down to the beach. He launched and shoved off, the morning star now paling over the sea, and the first grey creeping into the sky above the jagged mainland mountain peaks. The mysterious sound he had heard in the night still persisted: a low, sibilant murmur that seemed to come from the open water beyond the lagoon entrance.

Paddy shot his skiff through the pass. He took three more long pulls on his oars. Then, as his skiff glided into the clear, he leaned forward, frozen, mouth open while he stared in absolute amazement.

The water around his skiff was soupy with bait. Overhead, sea-fowl planed and wheeled in a white blizzard. And wherever he looked, far or near, the morning calm of the channel was marred and torn by the swirls of feeding salmon.

The big run had come! The coho were in! That was what had caused the all-pervading murmur . . . fish by the thousand, wolfishly attacking the bait! And those fish, those fine, fat silver-gleaming money-fish, were begging to be caught.

With trembling fingers, Paddy reached for the bait can in which his day-starting ration of minnows floated pickled in the formaldehyde mix. He made a foozle of threading the first minnow on his hook: did better with the second, and flipped it over the gunwale. Before twelve feet of line had peeled astern — even before he could slip on a sinker—a coho torpedoed his herring in an attack that doused his face with flung spray.

Paddy yarded that fish into his net, swung it inboard, and quieted it with a blow of his club. He rebaited and tossed out; and again, on the instant, a heavy, hook-nosed coho lunged to engulf his bait.

No sly minnow-skinners, these wild and hungry pirates that had swept down from the north! They struck close to the boat, and they hooked themselves solidly.

Paddy was netting his eighth fish when Mayus hailed him from close alongside.

"Hey!" Mayus hunched forward in a canoe laden with bed-roll and gear. "What gives?"

"The fish are in!" Paddy dipped his net and swung the coho, writhing and twisting, inboard. "You sure picked one heck of a time to pull out."

Mayus didn't waste time answering. He spun the canoe in its own length and, rowing at a racing clip, shot his craft through the pass into the lagoon.

Minutes later, while he skidded yet another suicide-bent coho toward his net, Paddy glimpsed Mayus tearing up the beach with packsack dangling from one fist and bedroll from the other. Mayus dumped his gear on the porch. He snatched up rod, net and herring rake from where he'd left them leaning against the shack—forgot his tackle bag and whirled back to grab it—then headed for the beach and his canoe at a gallop.

It seemed no time until Mayus was once more gunwale to gunwale with Paddy's skiff.

"Lend me some bait," he begged. "I threw all mine away."

Paddy reached Mayus his minnow can. He was only vaguely aware, while he tussled with another coho from the never-ending supply, that Mayus was also putting the blocks to a hefty salmon.

A hail, distant but shrill, swung Paddy's head around. Lynn, rowing hard, was driving her carvel through the pass. For once, they'd beaten her to the salmon grounds.

Raking bait was no problem on this fantastic first day of the big run. They didn't even have to kneel and peer from their boats' bows to locate herring. From where they sat on the rowing thwarts, they made blind passes with their herring rakes, bringing them up with silver asquirm on each needle-sharp tooth.

The salmon kept on hitting. Still skidding in coho, Paddy was only transiently aware that Lynn was rowing past him, inbound, with her slim carvel so burdened that it rode low in the water.

"Going to unload," Lynn called to Paddy. "You'd better too, unless you'd sooner swamp!"

Only then did Paddy realize what the morning bite had brought him. Fore and aft of where he sat at the oars, coho had slithered into wet and silver-gleaming piles from which jaw-gaped heads and broad black tails thrust at all angles.

Lynn was right: it was a case of lighten his skiff or risk foundering.

Pulling cautiously, with a wary eye out for each ripple and each shift of balance, he and Mayus eased their craft back through the pass and across the lagoon to the home beach. There they unloaded, toiling to and fro between the boats and the driftwood lean-to they'd hastily rigged to protect their catch from the sun. As a final precaution, they spread saltwater-soaked gunnysacks over the pile.

"C-come on!" Paddy urged Mayus, stuttering with excitement. "Let's go c-catch another boatload."

But Ben Hutchins called a halt.

"No you don't," he commanded. "Those fish ain't goin' anywhere. Not for a few days at least. Y' better save your strength for the evening bite. What we'll do is fix ourselves a meal, then you an' Lynn can run this batch over to the cannery."

Fingers hooked in belt, gazing at their haul, Paddy chuckled.

"You know that Chinese boy, Ben?" he said.

"What about him?" Ben asked.

"Well, looks like he won't have to go hungry!"

They forced down a rock cod lunch, vowing it would be their last, then dressed their fish — a massive job even with Ben's expert help. Then they toiled across to Bukwis cannery.

Joe Busby strolled down from the plant to meet them as they tied on at the float-string.

"So you hit pay-dirt," he said, grinning.

They fished again that evening with no less spectacular results. Again, they gutted fish until they could hardly see straight. Then once more, they wrapped cramped fingers around oar looms and, wearily, pulled with their second pay-loads of the day over to the cannery.

But Joe Busby offered an easement.

"No point in wearing yourselves out ferrying fish," he said. "While the run lasts, I'll send a gasboat over for a pickup every evening."

When they loafed their way back to Diablo through a warm black-velvet night punctuated by stars, it was with more supplies bought, including the meat for which they hungered.

"When we get home," Lynn offered, her carvel flanked by Paddy's skiff and Mayus's dugout an oar's length away on either side, "you'd better come to our place and I'll fry up those steaks."

"Great," Paddy agreed. "With spuds and carrots and green peas."

And gravy," Mayus supplemented, tone dreamy. "Plenty of gravy . . ."

126

"And a can of asparagus for me," Lynn added. "I've got two pumpkin pies out of the store freezer for dessert, and ice-cream if it doesn't melt." she laughed, sudden and low. "We'll have a real feast."

Funny, Paddy thought. *When she laughs, she sounds real nice.*

He laid his boat gunwale to gunwale against Lynn's sleek carvel. "Hey, Lynn," he said, "it was you who turned our boats loose, wasn't it?"

Lynn gave him a quick grin. "It was."

"And remember when you played ghost?"

"I'd sooner forget it," Lynn told him."

Paddy pressed on. "Someone was with you. Who was it?"

"My grandfather, of course. Now, will you shut up and row?"

Not for years had there been a run to match this one, Joe Busby told them when he pulled in to the lagoon in a company workboat next evening to take their catch aboard. Joe thumbed more bills—a generous serving of them—off a roll which he took from his wheelhouse ditty-box. Dog tired, but feeling good right through, Paddy added his share to the thickening wad in his jeans pocket.

"You keep catching 'em," Joe called as he revved his engine, "and I'll keep paying!"

With a grin and a flip of a hand he was away, leaving them to throw a meal together, then tumble into their bunks in anticipation of another big day tomorrow.

The run lasted all through that week and deep into the next. Life became first a dream and then a nightmare through which they stumbled and struggled, not turning in until long after dark, and out on the teeming waters again before first light.

They hauled fish until their hook-scarred hands threat-

ened to stiffen permanently into claws. They were welded to their oars. Mayus, plagued with a gurry-sore that came when fish slime infected a cut, rowed with a bandana wrapped around one hand. Even in his dreams, Paddy caught fish or cleaned fish or heaved fish into Joe Busby's workboat. They ate on the run, their food oftener than not no more than what they could grab up, and they learned to hate the sight, sound and smell of those rampaging coho salmon.

Meanwhile the fold of bills in Paddy's jeans became too bulky for a pocket to accommodate comfortably. Paddy transferred his stake to an old jam tin to which he added day by day. They were doing fantastically well: he knew that. Sometime when the fishing slacked off, they'd have time to tally their earnings.

The run came to an end as suddenly as it had descended on the Diablo Islands. One morning toward the end of the next week, Paddy came in with only a lone coho. That evening, he found the channel empty except for a pod of killer whales, shiny black-and-white monsters up to thirty feet long, that rolled with spiky dorsals high above the surface and with sighing exhalations of vapour.

For a while Paddy sat in his drifting boat, watching the creatures as they cruised in their lordly fashion. The bull's dorsal was so tall that it jutted above his back like a sail. He submerged to surface on the other side of the skiff, so close that the vapour drops from his blowing lay cold on Paddy's cheek.

The killers too, he had grown used to during this long sea-summer. They were huge, they were the scourge of seal and even sea-lion populations, but they never interfered with humans afloat.

Paddy sighed and bent to his bait can. He slipped a minnow on to his hook with a single, well-versed twist, and dropped it overside. Once more he dipped his oars, settling into a routine that had become as familiar as breathing. But no fish came, not even when the mainland hills turned smoky-blue, and dusk lay quicksilver on the channel. The coho that had swarmed thick as thieves for days past were gone, moved on to other waters.

Paddy absorbed the fact that the run was over with a curious sense of relief. Even though he knew that he had been performing a useful function — helping to put food on the world's tables — he was weary of fish-killing.

He and Mayus treated themselves to the unparalleled luxury of a sleep-in the next morning. They got up when the sun was high, fixed a leisurely breakfast of bacon, eggs, and hotcakes with syrup, and washed it all down with second mugs of coffee. Then, revelling in the prospect of a day ashore, they sauntered down to the beach.

Their boats were drawn up cheek by jowl above tideline, Paddy's battered and all but paintless ten-foot skiff, and Mayus's lean black dugout canoe. Each was silver-sequinned from end to end with coho scales. Fish blood had puddled and dried on the bottom boards. Clouds of flies buzzed around each hard-used, filthy craft, and they stunk to high heaven.

They didn't hear Ben Hutchins come down behind them. The old man's chuckle startled them, spinning Paddy around.

"Where's Lynn?" Paddy asked.

"Her ladyship's still poundin' her ear," Ben said. Then, "Look's like the coho fishin's over for another season far as this layout goes."

"But where do the salmon go?" Paddy asked. "What happens to them, Ben?"

"The coho?" Ben reflected, his faded blue eyes squinted as he gazed out across the satiny lagoon, "Oh, them salmon'll move on down-coast. Pretty soon now, they'll be headin' for their home rivers. They'll mill around in the crick mouths for a spell. Then, first good wet southeaster, they'll scoot upstream to their spawning beds."

"What happens after they spawn?" Paddy pursued.

"They die, that's what," Mayus put in. "They all die."

"That's right," Ben said softly. "The hen fish, she lays her eggs, thousands of 'em. The male sprays 'em with his milt. Then they bury 'em in the gravel to hatch next spring."

"But they really die?" Paddy persisted. "The parent fish all die? Seems like an awful waste!"

"Not so," Ben told him. "Their carcasses rot an' go back to the river to help feed the young 'uns around next April. It's nature's way with all the Pacific salmon. She gives the coho three years, then gathers 'em in."

They considered his words in silence which Ben eventually broke with another of his grunted chuckles.

"I got to admit it," Ben said, smiling at them. "You fellas did all right. You got fins behind yer shoulders an' webs betwixt yer toes, an' scales on yer necks. Ye row easier'n you walk, an' you think like salmon. You've turned into sure-enough handliners!"

Paddy felt a ridiculous surge of pleasure that reddened his ears and set him grinning. He was happy; and a new thought slippped into his head to add to that sense of well-being.

"You know," he said, "I just remembered. This is my birthday. I'm fourteen years old today."

"That's great," Ben said, and reached out to jolt his shoulder with a hard brown paw.

Mayus too was pleased. But he masked the fact by his gruff tone.

"Birthday or not," he said, "the day's wasting. C'mon, let's get these boats cleaned up."

13

Double Trouble

That afternoon they scrubbed out their hard-used boats, a messy and laborious job. But even after many buckets of seawater and much swabbing with mops improvised from wiry bunches of ocean-spray twigs, the skiff and the canoe still carried a haunting reminder of fish.

On their last run to the cannery, they had put in at the store to replace their tattered and salt-bleached clothing with new shirts and jeans. Now they made a small ceremony out of kindling a fire in the oil-drum stove and sending their old rags up in smoke.

"That's about it," Mayus said, half a stranger in the new bright checked shirt he had insisted on buying. "You know, I've gone up a shirt size. Must be all that rowing."

Paddy too had grown huskier in the arms and heavier in the chest. When he flexed, he could make a proper set of biceps. The work had been hard, even gruelling, but it had done them a power of good.

They dined sumptuously on pork chops, opened their last can of peaches for dessert, then set about packing their gear. Next morning, they'd be saying goodbye to Diablo... shoving off for Bruce Logan's ranch on Bukwis Island and for Mayus's home reserve, their handlining summer over.

The knowledge brought a touch of sadness. It had been a good and, finally, a rewarding summer, Paddy thought. One of his best.

"One thing we still have to do," he told Mayus, who bent above their driftwood table with a lighted candle set in a big white horse-clam shell.

"What's that?" Mayus asked.

"Count our loot," Paddy said. "And am I ever looking forward to it!"

Paddy fetched his bill-stuffed jam tin from under the loose floor board where he'd stashed it. He pulled bills from it, to make a heap on the table. Then, perched on a log round and working by candlelight, he set out to count his stake.

Mayus watched him for a while, then loafed out to the bucket on the porch for a drink of spring water. He returned with a full mug, which he set on the table at Paddy's elbow.

"Thirsty work, countin' all those dollars," he said with a grin. "How's she coming?"

"Don't think I'm going to make it," Paddy replied, head down and pencil stub busy. And a moment later, "No, darn it! I've only got six hundred bucks. If you want to be fussy, five hundred and ninety-seven dollars and thirty-eight cents." He frowned at the heap on the table. He'd done well, but not well enough. He was still over two hundred dollars short of what was needed to lift the load off his grandfather's shoulders.

"Damn!" he muttered. "I was sure I'd made it!"

"No sweat," Mayus told him cheerfully. "I'm kickin' in on the mortgage money too."

"But it's your own money," Paddy protested. You worked for it. That's not right..."

"Aw, shut up," Mayus bade him, the smile widening on his round face under the brush of raggedly-clipped black hair. "I got more than I know what to do with. Anyhow, us Bukwis Island Kwakiutl, we owe your granddad. He gave us an easement across his land that let us put our road through to the reserve."

"Well... Gee... Thanks." Paddy's heart lifted. He smiled back at Mayus. "You're not such a bad operator after all, for a lousy racoon!"

Mayus batted him in the chest. They grappled and rolled in a joyous clinch on the shack floor.

Behind him, as he squirmed out of Mayus's grip, Paddy heard a light tap on the door. Then the door creaked open on its makeshift hinges, and Lynn stood framed in the opening with the blue night behind her.

She too had discarded her worn jeans and shirt. She had on a white blouse open at the throat, tucked into a tan skirt. Her brown legs were bare, and her feet were cased in trim brown shoes.

Paddy and Mayus stared at her.

"Wow!" Paddy, knocked galley-west by the transformation, continued to gaze. "You look like a million dollars!"

"Looks to me like you've got about that much there," Lynn said. She spoke crisply; but as she nodded at the bills on the table, bright colour touched her cheeks.

"Not that much..." Paddy began: but the look on Mayus's face checked him. Mayus was staring past them, his smile gone.

Paddy's ears caught a subdued shuffle from the doorway. He swung around, expecting to see Ben Hutchins come to join the party.

But it wasn't Ben. It was Arnie Peters.

The creek robber stared back at him with brows tugged together. The tufts of hair that jutted up behind each ear from his otherwise bald head gave him more than ever the predatory air of a great horned owl.

Behind Arnie, face twisted in a grin, loomed Red Dunc Sloan.

"Well, boys." Arnie Peters' voice was smooth, with a hint of a purr in it. "We figured it was time we paid you a visit."

"Yeah," Red Dunc said. "A nice friendly little visit. You wasn't home last time we called around."

Red Dunc shouldered his way past Arnie. While Paddy and Mayus watched, Mayus propped on one elbow and Paddy still kneeling on the cedar-slab floor, he crossed to the table. Legs spread, rocking a little on his heels and with hands shoved into pockets, Red Dunc surveyed Paddy's hoard.

Then, deliberately, he reached out and began to gather the bills.

Paddy swallowed hard. Shock and rage restored his voice.

"You can't do that!" Only his voice wouldn't stay steady. It shot up in a falsetto squeak. "That's my money!"

"So?" Red Dunc continued to smooth out and pocket bills.

"The way we see it, what you got here is just about what we'd a' made out of that Cormorant Creek pink run." He pushed bills into his jacket pockets. "The fish you punks did us out of when you squealed to Mister smart-mouth Sorensen an' his buddies."

There was no humour in Red Dunc's smile. It widened into a fixed and chilling snarl. Arnie Peters stooped and reached. His fingers locked in Paddy's shoulder like claws. Wincing, Paddy felt himself hauled roughly to his feet.

Arnie cuffed him twice across the face—openhanded slaps that jarred his head and set his ears ringing.

"You stop that!" Lynn's voice was brittle with anger.

She stepped forward, Mayus at her shoulder. But Red Dunc half-turned, his bulk and his outflung arm checking them like a barrier.

"Thought we didn't know who turned us in, eh boy?" The owl-cruel face was close to Paddy's, the black eyes boring into his. "Thought you'd get away with it?" He shook Paddy savagely: he was working himself up to a pitch of violent anger. "We seen the two of you." Another head-rocking slap. "We seen you sneaking around on the beach."

"Ah, lay off him, Arnie!" Red Dunc had pocketed the last of Paddy's stake. Lynn made to push past him, but his big hand closed on her neck, squeezing until she gasped in pain.

In a casual reach, Red Dunc's hand went to the mug of water that Mayus had set out for Paddy. Red Dunc drank noisily, swigging down half the contents before he clattered the mug back to the table.

"Plenty of time to settle up with him later," Red Dunc said. "The way I figure it, we got only half their dough here."

Red Dunc turned Lynn loose with a shake and push that sent her staggering. His hand snaked out, locked in Mayus's shirt front and hauled him roughly close, holding him so that his feet were almost clear of the floor.

"Now, siwash," he said coldly to Mayus, "It's your turn to pony up."

"You can just go to hell!" Mayus's voice emerged in a breathless squeal. "And anyhow, it isn't here."

Red Dunc began to shake him. He shook, his heavy arm driving to and fro, until Mayus hung limp and dizzy in his grasp. "I know different," Red Dunc said. "Now you fetch it out, else I'll fix you proper."

136

Red Dunc's hand groped behind him for the water mug on the table. Still gripping Mayus with one fist, he raised the mug and swigged the last of the water.

Paddy's mind was working desperately. They were in a bad spot. He knew that he and Mayus might be lucky to get out of this bind alive. Arnie Peters and Red Dunc Sloan were tough operators — mean, ugly and vindictive. The kind who'd take pleasure into turning three kids into hospital cases, or worse.

Paddy's haunches were jammed hard against the table. Something was grinding into his flank. He worked a hand around, slowly and stealthily, and felt the outline of a small bottle in his hip pocket. He had this habit of jamming things into his hind pocket: that's where he'd filed his skull-and-crossbones bottle of formaldehyde.

If he could create a distraction . . . Get Red Dunc away from the door even for an instant . . .

Paddy dredged up his voice.

"Come on," he said to Mayus with all the conviction he could manage. "Don't be a fool! Give 'em that money."

While Paddy spoke, his hand edged into his hip pocket. His fingers closed on the poison bottle.

Red Dunc and Arnie were both staring at Mayus, who came up with a knothead answer.

"I won't. I'll not give you anything."

Red Dunc hauled Mayus closer and began to slap him, wide-armed swings that cracked off Mayus's face like pistol shots. Mayus's nose began to trickle blood. Arnie, watching, ran his tongue across his lips.

Paddy eased the bottle from his pocket. Groping behind him, he laid it label side up on the table beside the now-empty mug.

"Hey!" At all costs, he had to put on a convincing act. At his sharp interruption, Red Dunc stayed his hand. He swung his shaggy red head to glower at Paddy.

"You didn't drink that, did you?" Paddy pointed at the mug. He gaped in simulated horror at Red Dunc.

"Sure I did. What's it to you?"

For answer, Paddy jerked a hand at the table where the bottle displayed its bold black skull and crossbones.

"That water. It had formaldehyde in it. Deadly poison. I was mixing it to keep our bait fresh." He continued to gaze at Red Dunc in what he hoped was well-feigned horror. "Mister, *you've gone and poisoned yourself!*"

Red Dunc's eyes widened. He clapped a hand to his throat.

"Oh..." He swallowed convulsively. "Oh, Jeez, I can feel it..."

Red Dunc released Mayus. He lurched away from the door. "It's burning me..." He leaned both hands on the table, a man in the grip of terror.

Arnie moved anxiously toward his partner, widening the gap between himself and the doorway. "You got to take something, Red. Maybe mustard..."

Paddy jerked his head at Lynn.

"Now!" It burst from him with desperate urgency.

Lynn wheeled and darted for the doorway. From the corner of his eye, Paddy saw Arnie Peters lunge after her. Paddy dived for his knees, knocking Arnie off balance. Mayus cannoned into Arnie's ankles, grabbed, and hung on. Arnie staggered, stumbled, then crashed to the floor.

At least, Lynn had got clear.

What followed was a confusion of slaps and kicks that numbed the senses and bewildered the mind.

Hauled to his feet, half-fainting, Paddy heard Arnie Peters' savage voice through the ringing in his ears.

"I'm goin' to teach you, boy. I'm goin' give you a hot seat."

Arnie dragged Paddy toward the oil-drum stove, its sides still faintly pink from the last fueling.

"No... Don't..." Paddy dug in his heels, resisting with all his might. But still he was hauled nearer and nearer to the stove. He was so close now that he could feel the heat through his jeans.

"Come on, Red," Arnie panted. "Help me boost him up."

"I can't." The voice was hoarse, shaky. "I'm poisoned!"

"Like hell you are! It was just a trick. Lend a hand here."

Powerfully seized, Paddy felt himself swung high over the oil drum.

Glass shattered with a crash. Thunder blasted at Paddy's ears.

He heard a cold voice, swivelled his head to see Ben Hutchins leaning in the space that their shattered window had once occupied. Ben cuddled his shotgun butt to his shoulder: the muzzle looked big as a cannon-bore.

"Turn him loose."

Paddy felt himself released. He sagged to the floor. The cold voice continued. "Now, I got two more shells in this pump-gun. One for each of you. So you better lay yourselves down on that floor an' spread yerselves out an' don't twitch a muscle. Not unless you want a load o' goose-shot in yer gizzards!"

Red Dunc and Arnie hesitated, but only for a moment. Then, under the threat of Ben's shotgun, they disposed themselves meekly on the shack floor.

"Right on yer bellies," Ben growled. The ominous double-click as he jacked another shell into the chamber emphasized his words. "Legs spread. Hands behind yer backs."

The pair followed his orders.

"Now," Ben said to Paddy and Mayus, "git in there an' hog-tie them rascals. Lash 'em so they can't twitch a fin."

With vicious satisfaction, Paddy heard Red Dunc Sloan

grunt in protest as he took an extra turn around Dunc's wrists and, knee in his back for purchase, hauled hard on the length of rope he had slashed off a spare boat painter. Paddy knotted the line, then threw in another hitch for good measure.

"Just one thing more," he said, and plunged both hands into Red Dunc's bulging jacket pockets.

Red Dunc twisted his head to give Paddy a malevolent scowl. "We'll catch up with you again, punk. When we do..."

Ben Hutchins' shotgun muzzle, slammed into the back of Red's neck, silenced him.

"Where you're goin'," Ben said, "you won't be needin' money." He let the gun muzzle underline his point, fetching a yelp of pain. "An' ye'll be there a long, long time!"

Toiling together, they hauled Red Dunc Sloan and tightly-trussed Arnie Peters out through the doorway and stacked them on the porch. Though Ben Hutchins jeered at her for being a softy, Lynn spread a blanket over the pair to ward off the late-night chill.

"No use being cruel," she said.

"Cruel?" Mayus stared at the two, mouth pulled down. "In olden times, us Kwakiutl would a' took their heads!"

They stoked the fire, boiled up a lard pail of coffee, and with Ben and Lynn for company and steaming mugs in their fists, saw the daylight in.

Not long after dawn, a fishboat poked her nose around the south point. As the white hull eased through the lagoon entrance, Paddy recognized that tall and shapely silhouette. Gus Sorensen had come visiting in his *Wester-ly*.

"He's out early." Paddy watched as Gus dropped his hook, then swung aft to launch his dinghy.

"He's in a hurry, too," Mayus observed. "Wonder what brings him over here?"

"Don't ask me." Paddy raised a hand to massage his bruised and aching cheek. "I hope it's not trouble. We can get along without another dose of that!"

14

A Question of Country

Gus beached his dinghy and tramped up to the shack, a light-haired Viking with a tough and homely mug. Even though Arnie Peters and Red Dunc Sloan were trussed like turkeys, Paddy took comfort from Gus Sorensen's assured and capable presence.

Gus listened while they told him about the creek robbers' raid. When Paddy had made an end, Gus reached out a big paw and knuckled his scalp in the old, familiar way.

"You people did real well," he said. "Those monkeys should be out of circulation for a year or two." Gus spoke amiably, but the frown didn't quite clear from around his eyes. Paddy got a distinct impression that the troller man was worried.

"Something worrying you, Gus?" he asked.

"Well, kind of," Gus admitted. "Matter of fact, it's about you."

"Me?" Paddy gazed at Gus in surprise. "What have I gone and done?"

"I don't know," Gus said. "Only thing I can tell you is that the fisheries chief, Inspector Gillies, is pretty mad at you."

Paddy and Mayus exchanged dismayed glances.

"But why?" Paddy asked. "We've kept all the fisheries rules. Showed our boat-numbers good and clear..."

"...Didn't keep any little undersized shakers," Mayus supplemented.

"I just don't get it," Paddy said, his puzzlement increasing.

"Me neither," Gus said. "But anyhow, that's the way it is. That's partly why I dropped in. To pass on the inspector's message. He wants to see you on the patrol launch right away."

"I'll head over," Paddy said.

"Me too," Lynn said.

But Gus checked them with a flip of his hand. "Ain't all *that* much hurry. Give him some time to cool down. You'd better get some shut-eye first. You look all in."

"Sleep?" Paddy nodded toward the porch. "With those two out there? No way!"

"Well," Gus said, "S'pose I take charge of them? I'll toss 'em into bunks on *Westerly* and holler up the police boat on my radio-phone."

Gus stepped out to the porch. An odd reluctance kept Paddy and Mayus from following. The night's adventure had shaken them: they'd sooner not have to confront Red Dunc's snarl or Arnie Peter's owl-eyed stare.

From the sounds on the porch, Gus must have untied the prisoners' ankles and boosted them to their feet.

"All right," Paddy heard Gus order, sharp and rough. "Down we go...an' no funny stuff!"

Through the glassless window, Paddy watched Gus marching Red Dunc and Arnie down to the beach. He loaded them into his dinghy like baulks of cordwood, then clambered in and pushed off, so burdened that his gunwales were only an inch or two from the water. *Westerly* rode above her reflection in mid-lagoon. Not far from her, Red Dunc's and Arnie's ugly black drum-seiner lay at anchor.

Not till Gus had transferred the pair to *Westerly*, heaving them into the waist without ceremony, did Paddy breathe easy. He felt no goodwill whatever toward Arnie and Red Dunc. His face still hurt like the very devil from Arnie's cuffing. He hoped most fervently that they were out of his life for keeps!

Only when his head hit his rolled-up gunnysack pillow did Paddy realize how dogged out he was. He slept deep and dreamlessly, not waking until the sun was high and the shack like an oven.

A fast-looking grey Royal Canadian Mounted Police cruiser lay alongside *Westerly* in the lagoon. Paddy and Mayus rowed out. They told the corporal in charge about the raid. He listened attentively, asking questions and taking notes.

Finally the skipper-corporal snapped his notebook shut and rose from behind his swing-out desk.

"You did well, boys," he said. He gave them a brisk nod of dismissal. "We'll be in touch," he said, and that was that.

The police launch unreeled its wake out of the lagoon. *Westerly* loafed after it.

"Guess I'd better go over and see what the inspector wants," Paddy called to Mayus as he dipped his oars.

"You and me both," Mayus answered sturdily.

They had packed most of their gear the night before. All that remained was to roll and lash their blankets. This they did. Then, with their loads, they trudged down to the beach.

Lynn was there before them, her carvel afloat just off the shingle.

"You took your own sweet time!" she hailed them crossly.

One way or another, Paddy had been too heavily occupied for much thought about leaving Diablo Island. But now that the time had arrived, he felt an odd pang of sadness. He dumped his bedroll and rucksack into his skiff, then turned to stand gazing up at the shack.

It looked small, dilapidated and forlorn, with its staggering stovepipe chimney that they'd meant for weeks to true up, and its single blind window-space that fronted the lagoon. Beyond it, the other shanties made a lurching, strung-out ghost town. It occurred to Paddy that the handliners' camp on Diablo would be left to the mercies of sun, wind and rain.

And, of course, to Ben Hutchins, who for reasons best known to himself, preferred to make his home there. He'd be alone: Lynn would be using her coho-run money to pay her way into high school down-coast at Campbell River.

Life had been hard here. Hard, but deeply good. For those crowded weeks, the small grey hutch so haphazardly slung together out of driftwood had been their home.

Paddy took a last look at the shack, then in response to Mayus's impatient call, ran his skiff into the shallows and swung on board. Life went on. He'd better lose no more time getting over to Bukwis Island cannery, to learn what Inspector Gillies was riled about!

The fisheries patrol vessel lay long, grey and dauntingly official with its flag drooping in the windless air. Inspector Gillies stood on her after deck, watching as they approached along the float-string.

"You'd better wait here," Paddy told Lynn and Mayus: but both shook their heads.

"We'd better come with you," Lynn said waspishly. "In case brains are needed."

Inspector Gillies hailed Paddy from his stance on the deck.

"You took your time getting here," he said to Paddy. Crisply he added, "Come on board."

Paddy climbed over the side. Lynn and Mayus followed unbidden. They stood in a row in front of the inspector, who stared at Paddy, face set in harsh lines and frosty blue eyes like gimlets.

Paddy felt Lynn's hand reach for his. Her touch was comforting.

"You're American, aren't you?" The question, briskly put, hit Paddy like an accusation.

"Yes," he answered from a dry throat. "Yes, sure."

"Then you had no business applying for a Canadian commercial fishing license. You obtained that license under false pretences."

The inspector rapped out his words, each one landing like a hammer blow. "You've been fishing illegally in Canadian waters."

"But, Jeez..." Paddy felt his traitor voice betray him by climbing toward a squeak. "I didn't know that! I thought it was all right..."

"It wasn't." The inspector spoke with a rat-trap snap. He stood tall, straight and spare, every inch the impersonal representative of government. "It was a serious violation of Canadian law."

Paddy, listening, felt as if a pit had suddenly yawned in front of his feet. He'd never once thought... never guessed...

"But he didn't know," Mayus protested, coming lamely to his defence. "He wouldn't go breaking the law on purpose."

"Ignorance is no excuse," the inspector said. His voice softened a trifle as he spoke to Paddy. "Believe me, boy, I don't enjoy this. But certain procedures are required of us. Your boat is forfeited to the Crown. So is any sum that you received from the sale of fish."

The inspector paused. Then he said, "My department will be satisfied with these measures. We don't propose to lay charges."

"Charges!" Mayus spoke hotly and bitterly. "You've done enough to him."

Lynn had been listening intently, a frown grooved between her eyes. Now she asked a question, not of the inspector, but of Paddy.

"Where were you born?"

"In Portland," Paddy answered. "Oregon." He felt a curious numbness. This couldn't be happening to him...in trouble with the law, his boat and his stake confiscated, his season's hard work gone for nothing. He asked Lynn dully, "Why?"

Lynn ignored the question. She asked another question herself, darting it sharply at him.

"Where was your father born?"

Right here on Bukwis Island." Mystified, Paddy gazed at her.

"Then he was a Canadian?" Lynn pursued.

"He took out American citizenship later," Paddy said.

"But when you were born, he was still Canadian?"

"Yes."

Lynn whirled to face the inspector. There was eager triumph in her voice as she addressed him.

"Paddy's got dual citizenship. He's Canadian and he's American both, and he will be till he's twenty-one. Then he chooses which citizenship he wants to keep."

Inspector Gillies gave Lynn his sharp regard.

"You're sure of this, young lady?"

"Of course I'm sure. It was in our school civics course."

The inspector's expression softened a trifle. He sighed. It seemed to Paddy, anxiously watching, that his shoulders relaxed.

"In that case," he said, "I'm forced to assume that my department issued a license to the Patrick Logan who is a Canadian citizen." His grim features struggled against a smile, but the smile won. "It seems you're in the clear, lad. And so, I might add, am I." His blue gaze shifted to Lynn; the smile deepened. "We can both thank Miss Hutchins for helping us out of a painful situation."

They climbed back to the dock.

"You know," Mayus said admiringly to Lynn, "you oughta be a lawyer!"

Lynn said complacently, "Maybe I will be, some day."

Paddy looked at Lynn, too grateful for words. Still, he gave it a try. "I'd never have thought of that, Lynn. You're awful smart . . ."

Then words failed him. He halted, grabbed Lynn by her shoulders, and planted a kiss square on her mouth.

Lynn pushed him away. She gazed at him wide-eyed, in complete surprise. Colour flooded into her face. She turned and ran off along the dock.

Paddy stared after her in mounting dismay. *A dumb thing to do,* he told himself. *Now you've gone and got her riled. And after she helped you out of a jam!*

He walked on, mightily surprised both at his own impulsive action and at a discovery that impinged with startling effect on his consciousness.

She's pretty. Lynn's real pretty!

Sheepishly, he glanced at Mayus. But Mayus was elaborately ignoring him. He mooched along with his hands in his pockets, whistling tunelessly.

15

End of a Summer

Paddy stood by the wheelhouse of Gus Sorensen's tall white troller, looking up at the dock. His grandfather had surprised him by making one of his rare visits to the cannery for the express purpose of seeing him off. Bruce Logan paced to and fro across the splintery dock planking with his bagpipes cradled in his arms. He had been playing "MacRimmon's Lament", with many fine flourishes and grace-notes. Now he drifted into a plaintive air that Paddy could not put a name to for the moment.

Chief Simon and Ursula had also come in with Mayus to see him off on this fist stage of his journey home. The chief wore his ornate dance cape of red and blue stroud gleaming with mother-of-pearl buttons in the killer whale pattern.

Chief Simon held a dance-drum of rawhide stretched on a wooden frame. At intervals he tapped the drum with his fingers, so that the thudding paced Bruce Logan's piping like a muted heartbeat.

Paddy looked past the little group, hoping against hope

that Lynn would show up. But the dock approaches remained empty, and anyhow, there wasn't a reason in the world why she should come to see him off. Not after his performance of yesterday.

While Gus tinkered below-decks, Paddy let his thoughts rove back over their summer . . . the wild and wonderful time they'd had, and of the flash coho run that had turned failure into success. He tried not to think of the evil pair on the black seiner.

It had been like pulling teeth to persuade his grandfather to accept help with his mortgage. But in the end, Paddy had gained a reluctant acceptance. His grandfather would consider the money from Paddy and Mayus a loan, to be repaid when the price of beef climbed enough to make the sale of his prized Highland steers a less ruinous proposition.

Gus shouldered up from below. "All okay," he said cheerfully. "Guess we'd better shove off."

Again, Paddy's eyes searched the dock approach. It was silly, but he'd hoped, kind of, that in spite of everything Lynn would show up . . .

Westerly's heavy-duty diesel began its throaty pulsing. Paddy scrambled aft to free the stern line.

He looked up, line in his fists, to see a battered half-ton ease out along the dock. Lynn Hutchins swung down from it. She was wearing her white blouse and new jeans; her hair had the cedar-heartwood glow.

Paddy recognized the tune Bruce Logan played. It was "Will Ye No Come Back Again?"

Like an echo, Lynn hailed him from the dock. "Will you come back next summer?"

Paddy grinned. He felt right and good, at peace with the best of all possible worlds.

"Just try and keep me away! he called up to the girl on the dock.